D0115795

HIDE AND SEEK

HIDE

AND

SEEK

KATE MESSNER

SCHOLASTIC PRESS / NEW YORK

Copyright © 2013 by Kate Messner

All rights reserved. Published by Scholastic Press, an imprint of Scholastic Inc., *Publishers since 1920*. SCHOLASTIC, SCHOLASTIC PRESS, and associated logos are trademarks and/or registered trademarks of Scholastic Inc. No part of this publication may be reproduced, stored in a retrieval system, or transmitted in any form or by any means, electronic, mechanical, photocopying, recording, or otherwise, without written permission of the publisher. For information regarding permission, write to Scholastic Inc., Attention: Permissions Department, 557 Broadway, New York, NY 10012.

Library of Congress Cataloging-in-Publication Data
Messner, Kate.
Hide and seek / Kate Messner. — 1st ed.
p. cm.
Summary: For five hundred years the Jaguar Cup, sacred to the Silver Jaguar Society, was hidden in a cave on the coast of Costa Rica — so when a fake copy shows up on display in America, it is up to José, Anna, and Henry, junior members of the Society, to travel to Costa Rica and rescue the real cup from thieves.
1. Secret societies — Juvenile fiction. 2. Religious articles — Juvenile fiction. 3. Criminals — Juvenile fiction. 4. Adventure stories. 5. Costa Rica — Juvenile fiction. [1. Secret societies — Fiction. 2. Antiquities — Fiction. 3. Criminals — Fiction. 4. Adventure and adventurers — Fiction. 5. Costa Rica — Fiction.] I. Title.
PZ7.M5615Hid 2013
813.6 — dc23
2012027028

ISBN 978-0-545-41975-8
10 9 8 7 6 5 4 3 2 1   13 14 15 16 17
Printed in the U.S.A.   23
First edition, April 2013

Title page character illustrations copyright © 2013 by Yuta Onoda
Interior illustrations copyright © 2013 by Whitney Lyle
Author's note photographs by Kate Messner
Book design by Whitney Lyle

FOR BILL MESSNER, AND IN
LOVING MEMORY OF CAROL
MESSNER, WONDERFUL IN-LAWS
WHO HAVE ALWAYS KNOWN THE
POWER OF LOVE AND LOYALTY

ONE

The girl was small, but she ran faster than anyone in her village. And when the ships appeared on the horizon, she was the one called to the fire.

"It is time," the girl's grandmother said. She lifted a bundle, wrapped in cotton cloth.

The girl could tell it was heavy. She knew what it was.

She stared at the cloaked treasure in the old woman's gnarled hands, and her heart raced. She thought this moment would come later, after she had come of age. But it was happening now, and that could mean only one thing.

She was needed. It was time.

Her grandmother unwrapped the bundle carefully, as if she were handling the most delicate baby bird. But the creatures that appeared, glimmering gold when the worn cloth fell away, were the fiercest known in the forest.

A jaguar, all teeth and muscle and fire-filled eyes, stared out from one side of a smooth drinking cup.

A serpent rose from the other side, with thick, powerful coils and fangs that appeared to drip venom, though the polished gold surface was dry.

"They come. Soon — before the sun is gone — we will leave the village. We must travel quickly and will bring only water and food for today. Nothing more. Not even that which we hold most sacred." The old woman held the cup high so the girl could see brown glimmers of her own skin in its reflection. "This will not be safe with us. You must hide it so it cannot be found. You know the place."

The girl nodded. She knew. She reached for the cup, but her grandmother pulled it back. "First," she said, "you must drink."

Her grandmother turned, lifted a gourd from beside the fire, and poured its contents into the glowing cup. She held it out. "From this moment on, you shall be a sworn protector of the gifts of Ixchel, treasures of beauty and hope made by your people."

With trembling hands, the girl raised the cup. The horrible serpent faced away from her, but the eyes of the jaguar burned into her own as she brought it to her lips. The liquid inside was milky and sour. It warmed her throat, and though she knew it to be the fermented sap of the agave plant, somehow, as it filled her, it was more. The spirit of her ancestors spread from a place deep in her chest, through every part of her body. Her legs, her legs especially, felt as if they were made of the burning energy of the sun.

Her grandmother nodded slowly and reached for the cup. Carefully, she wiped the last drops from its rim, wrapped it back in the cloth, and placed it in the girl's hands. "You must go now. Be swift."

Clutching the cup to her chest, the girl ran the worn path from the village to the graves where her ancestors slept. She heard their whispers over the thump of her heart, urging her. *Go . . . Go . . . Go . . .*

She raced to the end of the path and beyond, into the thick brush, where branches tugged at her hair. Butterflies and birds erupted into color and squawks, startling from limbs and logs as she passed. Howler monkeys roared at her from above until finally she burst from the trees onto the sand and turned toward the cave. The tide was coming in, the water perhaps too high already.

She would have to be fast. She would have to be brave.

Waves rushed through the narrow channel to meet her, but she sprinted on, into the tunnel as if the light on the other side were all that she could see. It was bright, beckoning.

She made herself as tall as she could and splashed with strong steps into the darkness. The ocean's roar filled not only her ears but her whole body, down to her toes, gripping the sand even as it slipped out from under her.

Halfway through the tunnel, she stopped. Where was the foothold she needed? Already underwater? She wrapped one arm tightly around the cup and used her other hand to feel along the wall. Every wave surged more powerfully than the one before. Salt water splashed her eyes and licked at her face. But she held on.

There! She found the crevice at the waterline, jammed her foot into the narrow space, and reached up with one hand to pull herself higher.

Another wave struck her legs, and her toes slipped. She pushed them farther into the scratching rocks and found a narrow ledge for her second foot, just above the first.

The cup was heavy, and she was small. But she had made a promise.

In order to climb, she would have to let go of the handhold that kept her snug against the ledge, above the raging waves. She would not let go of the cup. She *could* not let go.

Instead, she let go of her safety — and for a breathless moment released her grip on one rock so she could grasp for another. In that heartbeat, she lurched backward, flailing. But then she touched rock again, dug her fingers into the crevice until she felt the slippery warmth of blood in her hand.

But she had to climb higher — well above the tide line of even the highest waters of the full moon — or the cup would not be protected in the darkness but lost forever to the sea.

She climbed — and let go — and clutched — and pulled — until finally her hand found the flat, smooth surface she'd imagined all through her struggles. It was here, in this crevice, she'd hidden the crystal-dimpled rock from her brother in a game of keep-away. It was here he'd been afraid to climb, and she had enjoyed his bellowing for a good long while before she climbed up again to toss the rock back down to her older sibling, who would not let his feet leave the sand.

Now, she pushed the cup from underneath, higher. Into the dark, empty space while the waves screamed below.

"Be well," she whispered. It was what her father told her whenever he left on a journey and would not be back for some time. "Be well."

She clambered down quickly — so much easier with two hands free — and landed in the rising waves. They pushed her back toward the beach, reclaiming their dark hideout. She nearly lost her footing with every staggering step.

When she stumbled into the light, she lifted her gaze. The approaching ships were larger. Soon, they would spit out smaller boats full of men with fair skin and hairy faces. They would land on the beach before dark.

But it was done. Clouds swirled above, reflected in the waves, and the rain began. Warm drops mingled with the salty air, tears from the sky.

The girl started back to the village, the home she would soon leave. When she reached the edge of the forest, she turned back to the cave and looked hard, as if she could still see the cup hidden high in its shadows.

"Be well," she whispered. "Stay safe."

And it would. For the next five hundred years.

TWO

José McGilligan stepped through the metal detector and froze.

He knew he'd have to go through security to get into the White House for this morning's reception. He knew there would probably be a metal detector. And that was fine. His secret wasn't made of metal.

But now some security lady was asking everyone to empty their *pockets*.

"Do we have to take out everything?" José blurted as his mother gently nudged him forward.

"Yes indeed," the security guard said.

"Okay," José croaked. He cleared his throat and swallowed, but his tonsils felt like cotton balls. He tossed his copy of *Pocket Quotations* into the basket, along with the small notebook where he'd been collecting presidential quotes to get ready for this trip. It made him feel more confident, knowing he had some smart words ready to go, even if he wouldn't be the first to say them.

And José needed all the extra confidence he could get on this trip, thanks to that envelope in his pocket. After his parents had gone through the metal detector, José took out the envelope and slid it into the middle of his quotes book, sending please-don't-open-that thoughts into the muggy June air.

The guard didn't open it. And his parents were too busy reclaiming the contents of their own pockets to notice.

"Ready?" His mother led them through a tall doorway into a wood-paneled hall crowded with reception guests and decorated with paintings of past presidents. Franklin Delano Roosevelt was huge and wearing some kind of cape.

"The only thing we have to fear is fear itself," José said quietly. Fear . . . and math class exponents that don't make any sense.

And that envelope, too. José hoped quoting bold, cape-wearing Roosevelt would give him some courage of his own. He had to tell his parents about the note.

He took a deep breath and tried to think calm, collected, presidential thoughts. The portrait of Woodrow Wilson didn't help.

"He looks all worried," José said.

"Yeah." His dad nodded. "World War One could do that to a guy."

The line snaked around a corner and up some steps to another hallway, and that opened into a room with a checkered marble floor.

"There you are!" Anna Revere-Hobbs came barreling up to José so fast she nearly sent him tumbling into a statue of Abraham Lincoln. "Ohmygosh, can you believe we're here?"

José smiled. He hadn't seen Anna in a few months, but she still talked as fast as she had on that crazy day he'd met her and another kid, Henry Thorn, snowed in at the airport in Washington, DC. Together, the three of them ended up tracking down the thieves who stole the original Star-Spangled Banner from the Smithsonian, which is why they'd been invited to this White House reception in the first place.

"And did you know the pre-Columbian gold exhibit is here today, too?" Anna went on. She never seemed to run out of breath. "And did your mom tell you about the Jaguar Cup? I am so excited to see it. Did they say yet if the president's in the building? I totally want to interview him for my school paper. My dad says sometimes he's here when people take tours and you might see him for a second or something. So how are you?"

"I'm good," José answered. "But I heard the president's not here. He's at Camp David. The gold exhibit should be neat, though."

José looked over at his mom, chatting with Anna's mother against the wall. When his mom told him about the pre-Columbian gold exhibit, she'd also shared more than he'd ever known before about the Silver Jaguar Society, the secret group made up of descendants of history's greatest creators — inventors and artists of all kinds. Those descendants had sworn their lives to protect the world's artifacts. José's mom was part of the society. Anna's mom, too, and Henry's aunt. Which reminded him . . .

"Have you seen Henry yet?"

"Nope." Anna shrugged, then lifted up on her tiptoes to scan the crowd. "Wait a second. That might be him." She jumped a few times, waving, until Henry ducked through the crowd with his aunt.

"Hey, you guys!"

"Let's keep moving, okay, kids?" Henry's Aunt Lucinda was a tall woman with a deep voice. When she said move, they moved.

They passed an enormous library. "Can't we go in there?" Anna asked their Secret Service escort, but he shuffled them right past the velvet ropes that guarded the doorway.

"So what's up with this gold exhibit everybody's talking about?" Henry asked.

"Your parents didn't tell you? I mean ... your aunt?" Anna looked down, quiet for once. Henry's mom had died of cancer three years ago, and he'd just moved from Vermont to Boston when his dad got married again.

"Nah." Henry paused. "Actually, she might have tried to tell me on the plane. I was playing Pirates of the Deadly Seas on my SuperGamePrism, though. I got to level nine."

Anna let out a loud sigh, but José laughed. "The show is an exhibit of pre-Columbian artifacts," he said. "Gold sculptures and necklaces and things like that from Central America, before the Spanish showed up."

"And most people don't know this," Anna said, her eyes gleaming, "but one of the pieces is this special Silver Jaguar Society cup and it's super symbolic. New society members would drink from it when they pledged their lives to protect their people's cultural treasures from the conquistadors — you know, the Spanish conquerors who traveled to Central America looking for gold and stuff?"

"Dude, I know what conquistadors are." Henry looked offended.

Anna looked skeptical. "Let me guess ... there's a video game?"

"Treasure Quest 1509," Henry said, nodding. "It totally rocks."

"Anyway," Anna said, "this cup was missing for centuries before archaeologists found it in a seaside cave in Costa Rica last year. But the coolest thing is that whoever left the cup there probably *saved* it from being stolen. The Silver Jaguar Society was famous for —"

"— for being *secret*." Anna's mother put both hands on her daughter's shoulders and lowered her voice. "It will *no longer be secret* if junior members crow about it in public places."

"Listen." José's mother motioned them in closer. Most of the other guests and visitors had gathered in the doorway of the roped-off China Room to stare at a bunch of fancy dishes. She whispered, "Anna is right. This cup *is* probably still around today because it was hidden. The earliest Silver Jaguar Society members knew the world they lived in — the mountains and forests and cliffs of Central America — better than the Spaniards ever would. They took advantage of that knowledge to spirit away many of the treasures the conquistadors were hoping to find. Statues of gold and jade were tucked into deep rock crevices or buried at the foot of ancient almendro trees. And there they remained hidden — and safe — until the threat had passed and someone was able to bring them back to the people." She paused. "These treasures told the stories of the people and belonged to them."

"But they didn't find this one until, like, last year?" Henry raised an eyebrow. "Those people musta been waiting a long time to get it back."

José's mom smiled sadly. "The Spanish explorers brought more than their supplies and weapons across the ocean. They brought diseases. In some parts of Central America, whole communities were wiped out. No one was left to go back for the treasures. Archaeologists found this one."

"All right, folks," a Secret Service agent announced from the doorway of the China Room. "If you'll proceed to the East Room, we can begin our reception, and you can have a sneak preview of our upcoming gold exhibit."

"At least the Spanish never found it," José whispered as he followed his mom into the room with the fancy polished floor. He felt better about the envelope crumpled in his pocket, knowing that some secrets stayed in the dark, where they belonged.

THREE

"This looks familiar," Anna said as they entered the East Room.

"Probably because you've seen it on TV," her mom said. "They hold press briefings here. Weddings and funerals, too."

"I wish I could cover a briefing here," Anna said, fingering her homemade "press" badge. She'd designed it on her computer to make it look all official, but the Secret Service hadn't been impressed.

"Oh, look!" José's mom pointed to a tall portrait of George Washington on the wall. "That's the oldest piece of White House art. It was here even before the British invaded in 1814."

"I thought they burned the White House then." José frowned. The painting didn't even look damaged.

"They did," his dad said. "Remember that piece of charred timber from the old White House we saw at the Smithsonian's Star-Spangled Banner exhibit this winter?"

"The White House burned," his mom said, "but the painting survived, thanks to the first lady at the time, Dolley Madison. Her husband sent a message telling her to evacuate when the British advanced. But she wouldn't leave until she was sure the Washington portrait would be safe for future generations."

"She took it with her?" Henry stared up at the enormous portrait. "Dude . . . she must have been one powerhouse of a first lady. That thing's big!"

"Huge. And it was screwed to the wall like nobody's business," José's mom went on, her eyes sparkling. "So Dolley Madison had workers break the frame and roll up the canvas so it could be moved before the British arrived. And here it is, preserved for us like Dolley intended." She nodded proudly.

"How come you know so much about that story?" José asked. His mom was an expert on historical textiles, but her knowledge didn't usually extend to art and other parts of history. Unless . . . "Was Dolley Madison a member of the Silver Jaguar Society?" José whispered.

His mom nodded smugly. "One of our finest."

They took their seats as the White House chief of staff, a short man with black hair and glasses, stepped up to the podium.

"Good afternoon, everyone. Four months ago, our nation was stunned and saddened by an unthinkable crime when the Star-Spangled Banner, the original flag that inspired our national anthem, was stolen from the Smithsonian Museum of American History. Today, our national treasure is back on display where it belongs, thanks to the courage and quick thinking of some young people who were snowed in at the airport on that fateful day. The culprits who stole the flag . . ."

The man spoke in a monotone, and José was sleepy. His eyes drifted to that portrait of Washington. If Dolley Madison could sneak something that huge past the British, his secret was going to be just fine stuffed in his pocket.

"Go on, kiddo." His father nudged him, and when José looked up, Anna and Henry were already on their way up front.

"The flag is so much more than fiber and dye. It is a priceless symbol with the power to unify us and inspire us to defy the impossible. It served as such an inspiration in 1814 . . . and still does today. So thank you, Anna Revere-Hobbs, José McGilligan, and Henry Thorn," said the chief of staff, "for your quick thinking and your courage." He handed them certificates, signed by the president.

And then it was over.

"Thanks for coming today. And if you'd like to have a preview of our pre-Columbian gold exhibit before you leave, head this way, through the Green Room and to the Blue Room."

"That was so fast," Anna said, turning to her mother. "Can I ask him for an interview?"

"Looks like he's already getting ready for the next event," her mom said, nodding toward the other door, where the man was welcoming a bunch of ladies dressed in red blazers. "Come on, you can write something for the paper about the gold exhibit."

Anna looked down at her press pass and sighed. Its edges curled in the humidity.

"Look, Henry!" Henry's aunt Lucinda charged into the middle of their group. "See the grand piano over there? It's a specially designed Steinway, a gift to the White House in 1938." Henry's aunt was a society member, too, who not only protected the treasures of history but seemed to know every single thing about every single one of them.

"I thought your dad was coming this time," José said as they made their way into the Green Room. It was full of chairs that looked way too fragile for sitting.

"He was." Henry shrugged. "But then he decided he shouldn't leave Bethany because she hasn't been feeling all that hot."

The next room was painted a gentle cream color, but the carpet and curtains were the blue of deep summer sky, and the walls were lined with softly lit display cases that seemed to glow.

José stepped up to a case full of animal sculptures — golden monkeys, frogs, and birds — and some creatures that looked half human, half jaguar.

"That is so cool!" Henry leaned so close to the glass his breath fogged it all up. "They're like werewolves, only . . . were-jaguars!"

José found a panel on the wall and started reading. "Culture and Columbus: Treasures of the New World features newly discovered treasures of Central America's indigenous peoples and priceless artifacts from the age of Spanish exploration."

"Looks like all the Spanish artifacts are big, heavy guns," Henry said, leaning in to read. "Hey! This whole exhibit's going on tour after it leaves here. Boston's next!"

"You guys, come over here!" Anna called from across the room. José's mom and dad and Henry's aunt, who had been chatting with a White House historian near the door, headed for the display as well.

José stepped up to the glass and bent down. "That's the Jaguar Cup?"

Inside the case, a golden chalice glowed with a soft shine in the display lights. Beautiful — but its shape surprised José. Instead of a simple jaguar as he'd expected, or even a human representation of the jaguar goddess, Ixchel, this cup had two faces: the gleaming eyes and powerful jaws of a jaguar on one side of the vessel, and on the other, the dagger-toothed head of a serpent.

José shivered a little. How could the sacred symbol of the Silver Jaguar Society also include the chilling image of the society's most notorious enemies? José had never come in contact with anyone from the Serpentine Princes, a gang of international art thieves, but he'd heard enough stories to make this image of jaguar and snake together on one cup impossible to reconcile.

When he looked up, his mother was frowning, too.

"Isn't that just . . . so wrong?" he whispered. "Why would they have a snake on there?"

His mother squinted into the case. "Because," she said quietly, "our ancestors who founded the society believed in balance. They knew that to ignore the darker side of humanity was to invite disaster, so this cup celebrates the jaguar, all that's positive about the human world, and at the same time, it acknowledges the existence of evil. Knowing evil — drinking from its cup — prepared them to face it with courage."

José's dad wandered off to another part of the exhibit, but his mom stayed. She didn't look up from the cup, and her frown lines deepened. She leaned over and whispered something to Anna's mom, and to Henry's aunt Lucinda, and all three of the women leaned closer to the case, staring.

They looked at one another for a long time, and finally, Anna's mom nodded.

Anna put her hand to the glass. "I wish we could take it out and touch it."

"Or drink out of it!" Henry said. "That would be so sick."

Anna nodded and whispered to her mom, "So if I'd been part of the original Silver Jaguar Society, this is the cup I'd have held in my hands — this very cup — to drink from at the ritual of initiation?" Her eyes glinted with excitement, and José could tell that in her mind, Anna was back in the fifteenth century with that cup in her hands.

"No," her mom replied, slowly shaking her head.

"But . . ." Anna tipped her head, confused. "You said the Jaguar Cup was part of that ceremony when —"

"Shhh." Her mother held up a hand.

"The Jaguar Cup *was* part of that ceremony," José's mother whispered into their tight circle while the other visitors thinned out, heading for the State Dining Room. "But this —" She looked down at the glowing gold in the case. "This is a fake."

FOUR

After they left the exhibit, José's parents and the other adults huddled in conversation with the White House chief of security for almost an hour while Anna, Henry, and José sat sweltering on the curb outside. Then came a flurry of cell phone calls, a quick walk back to the hotel to pack up bags, and the next thing José knew, they were being hurried into a taxicab van, bound for the airport and a soon-to-leave flight to Costa Rica.

On the way, José's mom did her best to explain why they were starting their investigation of the missing Jaguar Cup — the missing *real* one — so far from the exhibit in the nation's capital.

"White House security is as tight as it gets," she said, rummaging through her handbag. "We have an agent who'll do some legwork in DC, but given the way the artifacts were moved, it's more likely that whoever swapped the real Jaguar Cup for this fake did it before the artifacts ever left the Gold Museum in Costa Rica's capital, San José. We have some thoughts on how that may have happened, given what we know about one of the people who worked on the project." She pulled a roll of candy from her bag. "Anybody need a mint?"

"So . . . that means . . ." José couldn't figure out how the adults could possibly have learned enough about the maybe-theft in their hurried conversation back at the White House to know that it was a good idea for them to be winging toward Costa Rica. In fact, he was pretty sure it was a terrible idea.

But Anna was bouncing on the van's bench seat with her notebook, making the rest of them bob up and down as they veered toward the airport exit. "That means we're going on our first official Silver Jaguar Society mission! To the Gold Museum!"

"*We* are going to the Gold Museum," Anna's mother corrected her. "*You* are not."

"You kids will stay with Mom's college friend Michael and his daughter. They run a rain forest eco-lodge a couple hours from the city," José's dad said. "He's agreed to look after you until our work is finished."

Anna's jaw dropped. "You're leaving us with *strangers*?"

Henry's jaw dropped even lower. "In a *jungle*?"

"They're not strangers to me," José's mom said, smiling. "You'll love them."

"Besides," Anna's mom said, "society members have an understanding. They'll treat you like family."

"They're in the society, too?" José asked.

His mom nodded and started digging in her bag for money to pay the cab driver as he pulled up at the airport terminal. "Trust me," she said, hurrying José along to check his bags. "You'll be in great hands."

José sighed and watched a baggage handler slap a tag on his suitcase, bound for Costa Rica now. What was that quote attributed to President Truman? *An optimist is one who makes opportunities of his difficulties.*

Maybe José could make an opportunity of this. He doubted it, though. It was hard to be optimistic when you were jetting off to stay with strangers in another country where nobody would care about your carefully curated presidential quotes at all.

When they landed in Costa Rica, everything was a flurry of hurrying and waiting, shuffling in lines and through checkpoints.

"There he is!" José's mom waved to a man by the sliding glass doors. "Michael!"

Michael was shorter than José's parents, with black hair sticking out from under his faded baseball cap and an easy smile. He hugged José's mom and dad, shook hands with everyone else, and then huddled in whispered conversation with the adults.

Henry pulled out his video game. Anna took out her notebook — probably making a list of Jaguar Cup theft suspects, knowing her — and José slid his quotations book out of his backpack and sighed. His presidential quotes were no good now; he'd have to find some new ones, maybe from jungle explorers?

"All right, kiddos." Henry's aunt Lucinda came over a few minutes later and wrapped her big arms around Henry. "Michael's going to get you settled at the lodge. We'll be at an inn outside San José tonight. Our plan is to check things out at the Gold Museum this afternoon, talk with Alejandro if we can find him, and catch up with you at the lodge tomorrow."

"Who's Alejandro?" Anna asked. "Is he a suspect in the theft?"

"Don't worry about Alejandro." Anna's mom gave her a quick kiss on the head.

"*You* sound worried about him. You think he stole the cup, don't you? Who *is* he?"

Anna's mom ignored her questions. "Be good and listen to Michael."

José hugged his parents and climbed into the back seat of the van next to Henry. Anna sat in the middle, right behind Michael. It was the perfect spot for peppering him with questions about his lodge and his daughter, Sofia, who was ten and would be there when they arrived. José listened, looking out the window at the shops and street vendors, houses with dogs and chickens in the yard, kids walking along sidewalks with backpacks that didn't look all that different from his. He perked up when Anna's questions turned to the man their parents had mentioned earlier.

"So, Michael . . . do you know Alejandro?" she asked.

Michael's eyes narrowed in the rearview mirror as he looked back at Anna. "I know him very well. He's family, just like you."

José tipped his head. "But we're not really . . . oh! You mean Silver Jaguar Society family?"

"I do." Michael paused. Then he shrugged. "You might as well know. I'm sure Sofia will tell you all about him." He paused at a one-lane bridge, and a rusty pickup truck heaped with brown vegetables rumbled over from the other direction.

"Alejandro runs a cultural heritage center not far from our lodge," Michael said, easing the van onto the bridge. "He works with the Gold Museum sometimes, too. He was pulled into the society at a young age, when his parents went missing on an archaeological dig ten years ago."

Fat raindrops plunked on the windshield. First two, then three, then a steady, pummeling drumbeat. Michael slowed the van and flipped on the windshield wipers.

"Alejandro was eight years old then. He had no other family, so his parents' close friends, also society members, took him in. When they had to travel, he'd stay with another member. At first, everyone figured it was a matter of time before Mina and Roberto would show up, covered in mud, with a story to tell. But weeks turned into months, and then years. His parents never returned."

José's throat felt tight. Was this really a story to be telling kids whose parents had just ditched them to go on a society mission?

"So Alejandro ate most of his childhood meals around the tables of society members," Michael went on. "He drank their tea, breathed in their secrets and their passion. I remember one time —"

"But . . . it sounds like our parents think he might have stolen the Jaguar Cup," Anna interrupted, leaning forward. "Wouldn't he want to keep it *safe*?"

Michael hit the brakes and steered the van slowly around a fallen branch in the road. "He would want that more than anything," Michael said. "Sometimes, people have different ideas about what it means to protect something." He turned up the music loud enough to signify the conversation was over.

A lilting guitar and a woman's smooth voice, singing in Spanish, floated through the van. Anna leaned back and left Michael alone, and they wound their way along rivers and mountain edges, until the rain slowed to a steady, soothing rush.

The next thing José knew, Anna was poking him awake. "We're here! Open the door." She poked Henry, too.

Michael opened the van door, and they stepped out into the lobby of the eco-lodge. It had a red-tiled floor and pillars every so often to hold up the roof. But where the walls should have been were . . . well . . . walls of green. The rain forest grew right up to the lodge, and leafy limbs poked into the lobby as if the trees wanted rooms for the night. A gaggle of old-lady bird-watchers gathered with their binoculars near the edge of the forest.

"Look! It's a red-lored parrot!" one of them squealed.

Michael led the kids to the reception desk. "Let's get you guys checked in, okay?" He ducked under a counter and reached into a basket full of keys. "Anna, we're going to put you in the room right next to our bungalow, so if you need anything, Sofia and I will be right there." He handed her a dully polished metal key on a simple ring. "Henry and José, you'll be in the next room over, okay?" He handed them each a key. "Take a water bottle, too," he said, gesturing toward a box next to the desk. "We have hydration stations around the lodge where you can fill up with good clean water; that way you're not going through disposable plastic bottles all the time."

"Are they here?" a squeaky and excited voice called out from the office behind the desk, and then one of the skinniest little girls José had ever seen zipped under the counter. "Welcome, you guys! I'm Sofia and my dad told me all about you, and I'm so glad you're here because all we ever get usually are old people with binoculars and sweaty mountain bike riders from Europe, but that's only when they have the Adventure Races. Do you have all your stuff? Because I can show you where your rooms are!"

"Sure." José looked at the girl. Anna had finally met her match in the fast-talking department. And maybe in the news-reporting department, too. Under one arm, Sofia carried a journal thing that looked as well loved and often used as Anna's reporter notebook.

"Come on!" Sofia started down a path that led out of the reception area into the trees.

"Let them get settled, Sofia!" her father called from the desk. "Then you can swing by and get them for dinner at around five."

"Shoot," Sofia said, hurrying along. "I was hoping I could take you across the hanging bridge to see the real forest."

Henry reached behind him to untangle a branch that had grabbed at his backpack. "This isn't the real forest?"

"Nah." She laughed and pointed to her left, where the path forked off in three directions. "This is all secondary growth. The primary forest with the big old trees is on the other side of the river. Come on!" She turned to the right and half skipped, half walked onto a narrow bridge.

"Is this the hanging bridge?" José asked. It wasn't that big.

Sofia laughed. "No. You'll see the *real* bridge tomorrow."

José paused to look down at the gentle stream winding underneath them. The flowers lining its banks looked like something from a carefully cultivated indoor botanical garden — not plants you'd find growing on their own. He took a deep breath of soupy-wet air.

"Iguana!" Sofia called. She pointed at a branch maybe fifty feet off the ground. "See him?"

Henry squinted. "I don't see . . . Whoa! That thing is huge!"

José looked up. Sure enough, a fat, scaly lizard straddled one of the high branches, its brown and yellowy striped tail hanging off in a drooping curl. Its fat body glowed a shiny green-brown, and the row of thin curving spikes along its back made it look as if it might breathe fire any minute. It reminded José of the Hungarian Horntail dragon from the Harry Potter books. Only . . . real.

Anna took out her camera and snapped a photo. "When I get back, they'll have to do this issue of the school paper in color. I'm going to have such great stuff."

"Come on." Sofia pointed toward some buildings not far ahead. The path was covered here, like a board-walk with a roof. "Let's go see your rooms."

There were four rooms in each wooden building, up on stilts in the middle of the rain forest. "Does the river come up this high?" José asked. The water was off in the distance, through the trees, but they could hear its steady rush among the other forest sounds.

Sofia shook her head. "No, but when the rains come . . ." She looked at the swirling clouds overhead as she stepped up to a door. "Well, you'll see. The whole forest floor turns into a river. You'll be glad for the stilts then. The walkways, too, when it's time for dinner. Otherwise, you'd need to be wrung out by the time you got to the dining hall."

She tapped the door and said, "This one is our bungalow," then walked along the porch to the next one. A faded cloth hammock hung outside, next to a weathered rocking chair. "And here's your room, Anna." Henry walked on ahead while Anna reached for the door with her key.

"STOP!" Sofia hollered. "Don't move, Henry!"

She shoved José aside, disappeared into her own family's room for a split second, flew out with a long-bladed knife, and darted past them toward Henry.

What was she *doing*?

There wasn't time for José to call out or yell or anything before the blade flashed through the thick air, up and down — not onto Henry but onto a curled-up something at his feet.

"Holy cow, that was close," Sofia said, leaning the big knife against the rocking chair. "I am so sorry. We almost never see them over here — I mean, they're all over the primary forest, but not this side of the river." She shook her head and looked from Henry, who stood frozen, still obeying her "Don't-move-Henry" scream, to Anna and José, who cowered against the railing with open mouths, relieved that Sofia hadn't killed Henry but still wondering what had happened.

"What *was* that?" Anna said finally.

"This?" Sofia held up the knife. "It's a machete. We always carry them on longer hikes, but not around the property normally. I mean, it's been forever since we've had a fer-de-lance this close to the rooms."

"A fer-de-what?" Henry squeaked, looking down at his feet.

"Fer-de-lance?" Sofia said, searching their faces for recognition. "You don't know about the most dangerous snake in Latin America?" She motioned them closer. "It's okay. This one's no threat now. You can come look." She stepped aside so they could gather around the still-twitching rust, beige, and brown blotched body of a three-foot-long snake curled within steps of Henry's sneakers. Its head, next to the rocking chair, was a still, fat triangle with angry gold-brown eyes.

"It's called the three-step snake," Sofia added.

"Because you need to stay three steps away from it?" Henry's eyes were big. "Geez, I wasn't even two steps away when you —"

"No," Sofia interrupted. "Because if you get bit, that's how far you make it."

José swallowed hard. "You said you don't see them very often?"

"Not here," Sofia said. "Usually, they stick to the primary forest." She shrugged and reached for her machete. "We can go over there tomorrow."

"Sounds swell," José muttered, staring at the deadly, headless snake, still twitching on the wooden boards of the porch. He had zero interest in seeing the primary forest where those snakes usually live. Not tomorrow morning. Not ever.

FIVE

"Ready to get some dinner?" José asked Henry after they'd chosen beds and unpacked a few things. José had his Harry Potter collection and quotation books stacked on his nightstand.

"Go on ahead." Henry was obsessed with the in-room safe. He kept opening and closing it with the combination they'd been given with their room keys. "I'll meet you there."

"Fine." José put his key in his pocket and started for the door. He paused next to his backpack on the bench at the foot of the bed and thought about the envelope he'd shoved into the biggest compartment, way at the bottom. He didn't think Henry would go through his stuff. But he took the backpack with him, just in case.

Thunder rumbled over the river's rush. José followed the signs for the reception area, thankful for the covered walkway when the rain started. A few fat drops quickly turned into a downpour. José liked the sound. Costa Rica rain was louder than Vermont rain. Warmer, too.

When José got to the front desk, Michael was checking in a tour group — a tall, skinny red-haired lady with glasses on a chain around her neck, along with her flock of bird-watchers, all carrying binoculars. Sofia was already there with Anna, who held the office phone to her ear.

"So who *does*?" Anna said into the phone, blinking fast and scribbling in her notebook. "Well, yeah . . . but who do you think?"

"Is that her mom?" José whispered.

Sofia nodded. "Sounds like things aren't going well in San José."

"We're not going to do anything stupid, Mom." Anna caught José's eye and started scribbling on the paper while she talked. "You could at least tell us who you think might . . ." Anna sighed, dotted an *i* so hard she almost poked a hole through the paper right into the wooden desk, and slid the paper toward José.

No luck at Gold Museum.

Found Alejandro but no cup.

A. admits he sent phony cup to DC.

Says someone else swiped real one.

"Somebody stole the real cup from *him* after *he* stole it from the exhibit?" José whispered.

Anna held up one finger for him to wait. "So you guys are still coming here tomorrow?" She waited. "Okay . . . yes, I know. Okay . . . I love you, too. Bye." She handed the phone to José. "Your mom wants to talk to you."

"Uh . . . hello?" José said. The line was staticky but after a couple seconds, he heard his mom.

"José, are you there?"

"Yeah, Mom, hi. How's it going?"

"Okay. This is more complicated than we'd hoped, but we'll figure it out." She paused. "How was your drive to the lodge? Pretty wild in the rain, I'll bet."

"Yeah, there were some branches down and stuff."

"José, listen, there's a chance that . . ." But there was a hum of static.

"What time is the morning bird walk tomorrow?" one of the tour group men asked as he lifted his suitcase from the lobby floor.

"Six o'clock," Michael told him.

The man looked stricken. "Is there a later one?"

"Leo, if you want to see birds, you have to get up with the birds," said a short, wiry lady whose suitcase matched Leo's. "Now come on."

José turned away from them. "Mom? You still there?"

"I'm here. This phone line is not the best."

"You said . . . there's a chance of something?"

She hesitated. "Never mind. I need to talk with Michael, okay?"

"Okay." José looked up where Michael had been, but he'd left to take the bird-watchers to their rooms. "Actually, he just left."

She sighed. "Tell Michael I'll call later then. Sleep well, and we'll see you tomorrow."

"Okay. Bye." José put down the phone. He'd been hungry before, but now his stomach felt hollow and wobbly. He wished his parents were coming tonight.

"Leo, do you feel that?" The bird-watcher lady nudged her husband and looked up at the lights along the wall. They were rattling a little. In fact, the whole floor seemed to be trembling. A book jittered off the edge of a tiny bookshelf and thumped to the tile floor. Then the trembling stopped.

"Was that an earthquake?" Anna's eyes lit up. She was probably already writing a newspaper story in her head, and for some reason, it bugged José. It must be nice to look at every snake and surprise trip and natural disaster as one more headline possibility.

"It might have been a little one." Sofia shrugged. José almost laughed. It figured that a girl who cut deadly snakes in half with a machete wouldn't worry about earthquakes. "We get them once in a while." She picked up the fallen book and put it back on its shelf. "You guys ready for dinner? My stomach rumbling is likely to cause another earthquake if I don't get food soon."

The rain gushed down in buckets as they hurried up the steps to the dining area.

"Let's get a table," Sofia said, leading them into a wide, polished-wood-and-tiled-floor room that opened right out onto the river. José set his backpack on a chair and wandered over to check out the serving line. The food was simple — chicken, rice and beans, and salad. It would have looked good if his stomach hadn't been all twisty after that phone call with his mom. She hadn't sounded right. Maybe she was feeling homesick, too. He hoped that was all it was.

"Excusez-moi," said a man, reaching past José to fill his fat hand with dinner rolls. The man's belly pushed at the buttons of his too-small safari shirt as he sauntered back to his table by the river. His fanny pack had a price tag hanging off the zipper. The man sat down and poked a roll into his mouth the way José used to eat marshmallows when he was little, stuffing his cheeks until they felt all blown up and stretchy.

José filled his plate and followed Anna and Sofia to a table in the middle of the room as Henry came barreling up the stairs. For once, he didn't have his video game. He headed straight for the food, then joined them with a plateful of chicken and rice and looked around. "I can't believe so many people come to a place that doesn't even have televisions. No offense," he said quickly, looking at Sofia.

She laughed. "That's why people come." She pointed to the row of full tables by the walkway. "They're all part of a senior citizens bird-watching group. The couples by the bar are bird-watchers, too. So is that guy with all the dinner rolls. And see those two?" She pointed to a tall woman with spiky hair and a shorter man loading their plates with salad. "They told us when they checked in they're wildlife photographers." She looked toward the stairs and waved. "Hey, Dad! We're over here."

Michael headed straight for their table. "Hey, you guys," he said, but his smile was weak. "Listen . . . Did you feel that rumbling in the reception area?"

"It was an earthquake, right?" Anna uncapped her pen.

Michael nodded, his mouth set in a tight line. "It was. It didn't feel like much here, but it was actually a pretty big one. The epicenter was in San José."

Anna put down her pen.

José's heart felt like somebody was squeezing it. "Have you heard from my mom and dad? Is everything okay?"

Michael pulled out a chair and sat down. "They called back right after it happened, and they're okay," he said, and took a deep breath. "But the roads are all closed, so they won't be able to leave San José any time soon. The phone lines are down now — we were lucky to get that quick call in — but we should have an update tomorrow. Why don't you guys finish eating and try to get some sleep?"

"I've been thinking," Anna said as she flopped down by Sofia on the lumpy sofa in Henry and José's room. "It could be days before the roads are passable again, and that leaves us as the only available Silver Jaguar Society members to investigate the missing cup *outside* of San José. I mean, what if he's getting farther and farther away with it?"

"What if *who's* getting away?" Henry said, turning the knob on the room safe. He opened the door a crack, slipped his hand inside, pulled out his SuperGamePrism, and slammed it shut.

"Well, Vincent Goosen, of course." Anna shook her head as if she couldn't believe she had to explain. "He *must* be the one who stole the cup from Alejandro, don't you think?"

"Here we go again," Henry said, jabbing his thumbs at his video game. Some kind of crashing metal noise came from the screen.

José opened his thickest quote book; he needed some good ones to replace all his wasted president quotes.

Anna stood up. "You guys, I have this *feeling*."

José sighed. "You had a feeling a few months ago, too." When the Star-Spangled Banner had disappeared, Anna was absolutely sure that the culprit must be Vincent Goosen, the tall, slithery Dutch man who was the ringleader of the Serpentine Princes. "But it turned out Goosen had nothing to do with that theft, and I bet he has nothing to do with this one either."

Anna sighed. "You're probably right. But I feel like we should do something to help." She pulled her notebook from her backpack and turned to a fresh sheet of paper. "Okay . . . here's what we know so far." She wrote the words *Jaguar Cup* in the middle of the paper, then drew an arrow up to Alejandro's name. "Alejandro's job was to get the Jaguar Cup safely to Washington, DC. However," she said, drawing an arrow from Alejandro's name to a blank spot on the paper, "he felt so strongly the cup should remain in Latin America that he swapped it out for a fake one that could travel while the authentic cup stayed here. My mom says he admitted doing it, and then *someone*" — she drew a stick figure with a question mark for a face — "stole the cup from Alejandro. We need to find that someone."

Sofia bit her lip, thinking. "But Alejandro never saw who stole the cup from him?"

Anna shook her head. "He told my mom it was dark, and he was leaving the Gold Museum when someone grabbed it. There was no one around except a security guard. He says the thief came out of nowhere."

"Maybe the thief *was* the security guard," Henry said. "That's what happens when you get to round six in my Super-Heist Bank Robber game. The guards turn on you and team up with the robbers."

José turned a page in his quotes book. There were some good ones about the power of nature; they might sound pretty smart here in the rain forest.

"Henry, that's brilliant!" Anna shouted.

Sofia nodded slowly. "That would allow him to get inside the museum. Nobody would suspect a guard."

Anna bounced on the sofa. "We need to talk to Alejandro. Oh, I wish the phone lines weren't down!"

"Wait," Sofia said, "didn't your mom say Alejandro left San José after they talked?"

"Yeah."

"He would have made it home before the earthquake then, and home for Alejandro isn't far from here at all. We can go see him at the cultural center tomorrow."

"That's perfect!" Anna stretched her arms over her head and yawned. "I knew the society would need us on this trip. I just knew it." She turned to Henry and José. "You guys are in, right?"

"I'm in," Henry said, giving his video game a shake. "Darn. Batteries. I hope this thing charges okay tonight."

"José?" Anna tapped her foot.

José folded the corner of a page with a quote from the environmentalist John Muir. "Okay." He sighed. Visiting a cultural center sounded better than staying around here, waiting for some three-step snake to show up, or going hiking in the rain forest to look for one.

"Great!" Sofia said. "I promised I'd help Dad with the morning bird walk and then we'll go. You'll want to borrow some rubber boots for the hike; it's muddy over there."

"Over where?" José asked.

"In the primary forest," Sofia said, clearly enjoying the look of horror on José's face. "Didn't I tell you? The trail through the jungle leads right to the cultural center. We should see tons of snakes and spiders and stuff." She turned to Henry and José — "Sleep well!" — and headed for the door with Anna.

SIX

Anna, Henry, José, and Sofia were late for the morning bird walk. It was Henry's fault. He wouldn't stop playing with the room safe, opening it, closing it, checking the combination.

They arrived as Michael was leading a group out into the morning fog. There were thirteen of them — Michael, Henry, José, Anna, and Sofia, plus the dinner-roll guy, wearing the same uncomfortably tight-looking shirt, the photographer woman with the spiky hair and her husband, two of the older couples from dinner last night, and Leo's wife from the reception area. Leo had apparently decided not to get up with the birds, after all.

José noticed that Michael and Sofia both had machetes tucked in their belts; he hoped that didn't mean more snakes.

"So how long has everyone been bird-watching?" Michael asked the group as they started down the path.

"A minute and a half," Henry grumbled, wiping sleep from his eyes. José had heard him tossing and turning all night.

"Six years," said one lady. She gestured toward the other couple. "That's how we got to be friends. We took a class at the local community college."

"I have loved the birds since I was a young girl in Russia," said the spiky-haired lady. "My babushka could name a bird by its song."

"I, too, am a lifelong bird-watcher," the dinner-roll man said, nodding.

Michael led them around the lodge property for about half an hour, pointing out colorful, keel-billed toucans in the high trees and bright scarlet tanagers pecking at mangoes outside the dining room. He led them across the main road, partway up a hill, and set up his bird scope — a sort of fat, stubby lens that was like a cross between a telescope and a half pair of binoculars. "Let's see if there's any activity at the great green macaw nest this morning." He peered into the scope, paused, then stood and shook his head. "Still quiet. Want to have a look?" He motioned toward the scope and waited as everyone put an eye to it.

José didn't see much to look at — just a hole in the tree trunk where it seemed like maybe there used to be a branch. The dinner-roll guy kept brushing up against him while he looked, so José stepped aside to give him a turn. The man stared into the scope for a long time, as if he really wanted there to be a bird, and looked sad when he stood up.

"Have you not seen the macaws this season?" he asked Michael.

"Not here," Michael said. "This nest was active the past two years, though, so we're hoping."

"You've seen them elsewhere?" The man looked around. "Nearby?"

Michael picked up the scope and started back down the hill, toward the lodge. "In other trees, yes, but not in areas as safe as this one, so we don't share their locations. If you really want to see a great green macaw, you can sign up for one of the educational programs at the wildlife center in town. They have several they've been working to rehabilitate."

"Feh," the man said. "That is no good."

"I know . . . not the same as seeing them in the wild." Michael shrugged and smiled. "But I bet you've already added some great birds to your list this week, no?"

"What?" The man stopped so quickly that Anna almost crashed into him.

"Your life list? Don't you keep a list of all the birds you've seen?" Michael looked back over his shoulder, and the man's face relaxed. "I bet you've seen new ones on this trip."

"Oh, yes . . . yes." The man started walking again. "The . . . eh . . . toucans and . . . eh . . ." José saw him pull one of the narrow bird brochures from his shorts pocket and peek down at it. "And the resplendent quetzal . . . absolutely beautiful."

"You saw a quetzal?" Michael asked, putting his scope down on one of the benches when they arrived back at the reception area. "Where?"

"Oh, it was . . . ah . . . on a morning walk here," the man said. "First day."

"What? That's . . . Who was your guide?"

"Oh, no guide." The man waved his hand in front of his face as if he could erase the words from the air. "Just . . . on my own . . . I see it in the trees and identify."

"Wow. That's . . . unusual." Michael gave him a curious look, then turned to the rest of the group. "Thanks for joining us this morning. We'll see you tomorrow — same time."

The other adults headed for breakfast, but the dinner-roll guy lingered. "Do you think," he asked, sidling up to Michael, "that tomorrow, we might . . . ah . . . take a trip to the other green macaw nest?"

"I'd love nothing more than for you to have that bird on your list, but as I mentioned, the local preservation group has agreed to protect the location of the other nests."

"Ah . . . but we are friends, no?" The man smiled and put an arm around Michael. One of his shirt buttons popped off and rolled under the bench.

Michael smiled and bent to pick it up. "Of course, my friend, but surely as a bird lover, you understand how we need to protect these beauties." He handed the man his button. "I'll have housekeeping bring you a sewing kit. And perhaps we could arrange a zip line tour for you this afternoon instead? It's a great thrill, and Luci can book it for you."

The man harrumphed, but he headed off to see Luci at the reception desk.

Michael turned to the kids. "I'm hoping we'll hear good news from San José later. The cleanup seems to be coming along, and I know your folks will call as soon as they can. Any plans today?"

"We're going to go see —" Anna started, but Sofia interrupted her.

"The glass frog." Sofia reached under the reception desk and started pulling out pairs of rubber boots.

"Here you go." She handed some to José, and he put them on. They felt all big and damp and shadowy, like there'd be room for his feet and a bunch of bugs and spiders. He wiggled his toes and tried not to think about it.

"Why'd you tell him we were going to look for some frog?" Henry asked as they trudged past the lodge swimming pool. "Aren't we going to see Alejandro?"

"Yep. But Alejandro's still technically under investigation for the Jaguar Cup thing, so if I'd told my dad we were going to see him . . ."

"It's easier to ask forgiveness than it is to get permission," José mumbled.

"You said it." Sofia smiled.

"Actually," José said, "I didn't say it first. It's a quote, attributed to Grace Hopper."

"Oh." She looked at him, then quickly glanced away, up at the sky.

"She was a Navy officer and pioneering computer scientist," José went on. "She was a real —"

"Sloth!" Sofia pointed to one of the tall trees. "See it?"

"Oh, yeah!" Anna took out her notebook and jotted it down.

Henry made a face at her. "Dude, you brought your notebook to the jungle?"

"Didn't you bring your video game?"

"That's different."

"It is not. Besides, I'm keeping a list of everything I see in case I want to do a sidebar on the wildlife to go with my story about the Jaguar Cup." She tucked the notebook back into her pocket. "Sofia carries a notebook, and she lives here. It can't be that uncool."

Sofia was leaning against the pool fence, sketching. "I like to draw him." She looked up at the tree, then down again and drew in some fur. "Or her. I can't really tell. That sloth is always in this tree. Usually, it just looks like a furry blob up there."

"Can I see?" José asked, leaning over to check out her drawing.

Sofia blushed and held it up. Her hand shook a little, but José couldn't imagine why she'd be nervous to share the sketch. It was really good.

"I like the way you drew his claws on the branch," he said. "Or, you know, her claws."

"Thanks." She put the notebook away and started up a path through some low bushes. "The bridge is up here." They followed her up an incline.

"*This* is the bridge?" José said.

No. Bridges were strong, sturdy structures made of steel and concrete. This green, wiry-looking thing looked as if someone had strung it between the riverbanks as a line for drying laundry. The bridge was made of metal, but it was skinny, wimpy metal that might as well have been braided sewing thread, as far as José was concerned. The railing that was supposed to keep them safe was no bigger around than his thumb, and you could peer right down through the thin grate that crossed the river. It certainly didn't look like something you'd walk on. But Sofia was already ten steps out.

No one followed her. Not even Anna.

"Dude, how old is this thing?" Henry asked, easing a boot out onto it.

"It's brand new," Sofia said proudly. "Last summer, the river washed the old one clear away." She gave a little bounce. The whole bridge pulsed up and down with her. "Come on!"

Henry took a step. He hesitated but then took a deep breath and walked slowly out to the middle of the bridge to stand with Sofia.

Anna stepped out, too, taking little sideways shuffles — step-slide, step-slide — until she met them. "Can we just keep going? Because I'm going to freak if I look down." Sofia stepped to one side so Henry and Anna could finish crossing.

"Come on, José. It's perfectly safe." Sofia held the two thin rails on either side and jumped a couple times to prove it. She bounced and the bridge bounced, but nothing broke into a million pieces and got washed clear away, so even though José's stomach lurched, he got a good grip on the railings and started sliding his feet, one in front of the other, in the least bouncy way possible, across the bridge.

He held his breath the whole way and let it out in a big whoosh on the other side.

"Follow me," Sofia said, and slid halfway down the muddy bank of a tiny stream that fed the river. Anna, Henry, and José slipped down to stand next to her while she gently turned over leaves on a bush, one by one, until she found what she was looking for. "Look!" she cried, holding the leaf gently.

José didn't want to be rude, but it didn't look all that impressive.

"Snot?" Henry scoffed. "We crossed the swinging bridge of death and slid down this bank so you could show us snot on a bush?"

"Wait . . . they're . . . are they eggs?" Anna leaned in closer, and so did José. Sure enough, there were tiny, round, yellowish specks in the snot. There were two blobs of it, and one of them . . .

"Ohmygosh, it's a frog!" Anna exclaimed, so excited she lost her balance and stumbled backward over a fallen tree.

"Bees!" Henry screamed, scrambling up the bank. José's heart just about stopped when he saw the swarm pouring out of that log. And Anna was right there in the middle of them!

"Anna!" Without thinking, José took a step toward her and held out a hand to pull her up. He squeezed his eyes closed, expecting to feel the stings on his bare forearm any second. But the stings never came. And Anna never grabbed his hand. When he opened his eyes, he saw Sofia laughing, in the middle of the swarm, helping Anna to her feet and wiping mud off her cheek.

"They're stingless bees." Sofia stuck her hand right in the middle the swarm as if she were waiting for a butterfly to land on it. "All buzz and no bite."

"Oh." José's hands were still shaking. He stepped back to the bush and pretended to look at that frog on the leaf while his heart settled.

"This guy's a male glass frog," Sofia said. "He's been here the past five or six days, guarding the eggs."

"You can hardly see him at all," Anna said, her voice full of wonder. "This guy is *so* going in my article."

"He blends in," Sofia said, "like a lot of wildlife here. They hide in plain sight."

José wondered what else they'd stumble on, hiding in plain sight. Bees *with* stingers? Killer snakes? Giant spiders? He wanted to get this walk over with. "Maybe we should check on Henry," he said, and started up the bank. At the top, Henry leaned against a tree, still trying to catch his breath after running from the stingless bees. Sofia and Anna left the snot-frog to guard his eggs and climbed up, too.

"You know, that was pretty brave," Sofia said quietly, glancing over at José as they climbed.

"Huh?"

"You tried to help Anna. I knew those bees wouldn't sting me. You didn't, but you rushed in there anyway."

"Oh . . . well, yeah. Thanks."

"Ready to get going?" Sofia asked when they reached Henry. She led them down the main path away from the bridge, veering to one side of the trail to avoid a loose pile of dirt. "Watch that," she said. "Those'll give you a heck of a bite."

José jumped aside, just as two of the biggest, fattest black ants he'd ever seen emerged from the hill. They looked hungry enough to eat him, bones and all.

"Let me guess," Henry said, giving the ants plenty of space. "Four-step killer ants?"

"No." Sofia laughed. "We actually call these twenty-four-hour ants. Or bullet ants. Alejandro got stung once and said it's a perfect name. He was in agony for a full day and night — said it felt like somebody shot him in the leg." Sofia started walking again. "There's a tribe in Brazil that actually uses bullet ant stings as part of their initiation rites for warriors."

"Well, cross that career goal off my list," Henry said.

"No kidding." José took a deep breath and started walking with one last, longing look behind them. In a forest full of three-step snakes and bullet ants, the snot frog and stingless bees were looking better all the time.

SEVEN

They never saw a fer-de-lance on the trail — only a hog-nosed viper that Sofia said was venomous but not aggressive. She pulled out her notebook and took a few seconds to sketch its smooth coils.

"Ready? We can walk around him," she said.

"Walk *around* him?" Henry shook his head. "What about your machete?"

Her mouth dropped open in disgust. "Henry! This forest is *his* home, not ours. The only time I ever, *ever* kill a snake is if someone's in real, immediate danger. And you're not. So come on." She skipped past the snake.

Henry held his breath and followed her, giving the snake plenty of space.

Soon, the trail widened and opened into a broad clearing with a round, brick-colored building and an overhanging thatched roof. A mud-spattered motorbike leaned against the wall.

"Oh good!" Sofia said. "Alejandro's here!" Anna, Henry, and José followed her to the door and stepped inside. José had been expecting something simple and rustic, based on the building, but inside, the circular room gleamed with well-lit glass display cases along the curved walls.

"Hmm . . ." Sofia said, peering around. The room was wide open — and empty. "He's not here. But you guys can look around. He won't care, and I'm sure he'll be back soon."

José stepped into the big round room, a cave of clean quiet in the middle of the squawks and buzz of the forest outside. "Are you sure this is okay?" Back in Washington, DC, all the museums had been staffed, guarded, and crowded.

"It's fine," Sofia said, strolling along one curving wall. "Come see the Danza de los Diablitos masks Alejandro makes."

José followed her past a display of traditional costumes and carved jicama gourds to a display case of colorful masks. One looked like some kind of king, with a long blue face, bright orange eyes, and twisted horns. Another mask had two frogs — yellow-green and blue — perched on branches above the eyeholes. And one was the color of sand and looked as if jungle vines or snakes were wrapped around the face; haunted eyes peered out from the coils. Two regal green-and-red birds perched at the top of that one. José leaned in to read the informational plaque mounted on the wall beside it: *Boruca Mask, carved balsa wood. Resplendent Quetzal.*

"Isn't that the bird your dad got all excited about this morning? When that guy said he'd seen one?" José asked.

Sofia scoffed. "Yeah, only there's no way he saw that bird. We've never logged one here; they're even hard to spot up in the cloud forest at Monteverde."

"Wow," Henry said, leaning in to look at the devil-looking mask. "I wouldn't mess with that guy."

"That's the idea," Sofia said. "These masks are for Danza de los Diablitos — Dance of the Little Devils." She pointed to another informational plaque that described the annual Costa Rican tradition and started reading aloud. "Danza de los Diablitos is a three-day festival in which the men of the Boruca tribe act out a violent fight between the Spanish conquerors and the indigenous people. The Spanish are depicted by a dancer in a bull costume made of burlap and a horned balsa mask, while the indigenous people wear devil masks."

"So they reenact the Spanish conquest every year?" José asked. "That seems like a weird thing to celebrate."

"Yeah." Henry scrunched up his nose. "Why would you want to reenact getting your butt kicked?"

"Because you get to write your own ending," Sofia said. "In Danza de los Diablitos, the fighting goes on three days, and then the indigenous people win. The whole thing is full of symbolism. They slay the bull and auction off its . . . well . . ." She pointed to the last paragraph of the description, then rushed off to look at ceremonial dresses with Anna.

Henry leaned in to read. "Holy cow!"

"No . . . not cow. Bull . . . otherwise it wouldn't have that . . . er . . . part to auction off." José laughed and walked along to look at the rest of the masks. There were dozens and dozens, and each one was so detailed. It must have taken Alejandro years to carve them all.

"You like the masks?" A young man called as he

walked in from outside. He wore rubber boots, and his pants were slick with reddish mud.

"Alejandro!" Sofia ran up to him.

"*¡Diablito! ¿Qué pasa?*" He smiled and reached out to muss her hair, then glanced behind him, out the door. They talked back and forth in Spanish a little. José could only pick out a few words — *friends, mother, father* — he guessed she was telling Alejandro who they were. He nodded but kept looking outside.

"Are you getting a tour bus today?" Sofia asked in English.

"What? Oh, no . . . no. Sorry." Alejandro turned quickly back to her and José. "Sofia tells me you're friends of her family."

"Kind of, yeah," José said. He couldn't quite get over the fact that the legendary Alejandro — who had grown up at the table of the Silver Jaguar Society after his parents died in its service, who had dedicated his life to its cause, who had carved all those angry masks — just looked like a regular teenager.

Tires crunched on the gravel driveway outside, and Alejandro startled. "Ah . . . I have another visitor. You should probably be heading home, yes?"

Sofia shook her head. "No, we want to talk to you. We can wait till you're done."

A car door slammed. Alejandro shifted his weight from foot to foot. "Well . . . I may be a bit." With a quick hand on José's shoulder and one on Sofia's, Alejandro herded them to the far side of the room and pressed the button on an old VCR attached to a monitor. "Show your friends that short history video for the region," he told Sofia, glancing once more at the door as he pressed PLAY. "The artifacts they see here will mean so much more then. I will take care of my business, and then we will talk." Steel drum music played from the monitor's speakers. Alejandro turned it up louder and hurried out the door.

"Soon after the Spanish conquest . . ." a narrator's voice began.

Henry reached into his back pocket and pulled out his GamePrism.

Anna settled into her chair and started taking notes from the video.

But Sofia was staring at the empty doorway, her eyebrows furrowed. Even over the loud documentary narrator, voices drifted in the window across the big round room. At least one of the voices was a woman, and she didn't sound happy.

"Who do you think he's talking to out there?" José asked. He was starting to understand why his parents had suspected Alejandro in the first place.

Sofia shrugged, then stood and moved so her back was to the wall. She motioned for José to come, too. Anna looked up, put down her notebook, and joined them.

Henry kept playing his game, legs stretched out in front of him. His thumbs poked at the game screen like woodpecker beaks, but the rest of him was settled in like that sloth by the pool.

Sidestepping their way around the curved wall so they couldn't be seen from outside, Anna, José, and Sofia slithered to the window. Sofia ducked down, scrambled under it, and popped up on the other side. José crouched below the window, and Anna hovered at the edge of the casing.

"Your promises you have not kept," a woman's voice said.

"My friend." That was Alejandro. "Some things are not in my control. And I apologize. But I am a man of my word, and you shall . . ." His voice faded into a mumble.

"What did he promise her?" Anna whispered.

"And who *is* that lady?" José hissed.

Slowly, Sofia inched forward so she could peer out the window. She blinked, then ducked back quickly. "It's the Russian woman from the lodge. He's showing her a map."

"In these caves," the woman said, "I had better find what you promise."

"You will . . . but I must ask that you make payment now."

Their voices quieted, or maybe José's heart was pounding so hard it drowned them out. "You guys," he hissed and frantically gestured them away from the window so he wouldn't be heard. His forehead was damp from the hot, moist air, and from squatting so long under the window with no breeze. And his racing thoughts seemed to be stealing away his breath. "Sofia . . . What if Alejandro lied to our parents about why he stole the Jaguar Cup? About it being swiped from under his nose? What if he's had it the whole time?"

She shook her head slowly. "You don't know Alejandro," she said. "That's not possible. He would never —"

The voices outside rose again, and Sofia darted back to the window to peer out. José got there in time to hear Alejandro say, "Here . . . here is where you will find what you seek. And then you will pay the rest."

José lifted his head high enough to watch the woman fold a highlighted map into quarters and tuck it into her back pocket. Then she pulled a thick roll of cash from her fanny pack and handed it to Alejandro, who shoved the cash into his pants pocket.

"Did you see that?" he hissed down at Anna and Sofia. "She gave him a ton of money."

Sofia shook her head as if a mosquito were bothering her. Or a thought she didn't even want to consider. "That doesn't mean anything. He does ecotours. He might have taken her on a . . . a bird-watching trip or . . ."

"In a cave?" José whispered. "They were talking about a cave."

"Well, maybe . . ." She shook her head again. "We need to hear his side of this story."

"You guys, she's leaving. And he's coming." Anna ducked down and hustled back to the corner with the VCR as the Jeep's engine revved. They slid into their seats as Alejandro came striding through the door. The credits were rolling on the video screen, and Henry let out a sharp sigh.

"Shoot," he said. "I was eighty points away from the high score." He looked up at José, Anna, and Sofia, half out of breath in their seats, then up at Alejandro, standing beside them with his hands on his hips.

"So," Alejandro said, raising his eyebrows. "What did you want to talk to me about?"

EIGHT

"We were wondering . . ." Sofia's voice was like thin soup. "How well did you see the security guard the night the Jaguar Cup was stolen?"

Alejandro drew in a whistle of breath between his lips. "Your parents told you how it all happened?"

Sofia shook her head. "Not really. They said you switched the real cup for a fake one. And then somebody stole the real one."

"More or less." Alejandro shook his head. "I'm so angry at myself. But I . . . somehow, I couldn't let it go on tour. It had been lost for so long."

He pushed his hands into his pockets and looked down, rocking on his feet. José wondered if his fist was clenched around that wad of cash he'd stuffed in there a few minutes ago.

Alejandro looked up — he was either totally distressed or a totally great actor — and his voice trembled. "The Jaguar Cup belongs to the people. It always has. It belongs *here*. So when it was time for me to pack it up, I . . . I packaged the replica I'd made for the cultural center instead. I wrapped the real one up in my rain jacket, and . . ." He shook his head and swallowed hard. "I was going to bring it back here where it would be safe."

"Safe?! This place doesn't have any security at all!" Henry exclaimed.

"This place is in the middle of the jungle, and nothing on display here is of great value." He glanced around. "Some old dresses, a few carved gourds, a bunch of masks. It was the perfect place to hide a treasure — in plain sight. Hardly anybody comes here unless a tour bus gets lost." He sighed. "But I never made it. When I walked out of the Gold Museum in San José that night, somebody jumped me."

Anna held her pen over her notebook. "You . . . didn't see who?"

He shook his head. "There was nobody around; that's the weird thing. I mean, I'm not stupid. When I stepped out, I scanned the whole block. I knew what I was carrying, and I wasn't going to take any chances. The place was dead quiet except for a security guard smoking by the back door."

"Well, did he notice anything?" José asked.

Alejandro shrugged. José could see the wad of money bulging in his pocket.

Anna tapped her pen against her cheek, frowning. "Didn't the police interview that security guy?"

Alejandro shook his head.

"Why not?" Anna looked as if she might steal Alejandro's motorbike and ride it to San José to give those police a good lesson in questioning, but then her face sank with understanding. "You never told them."

Alejandro looked at his watch. "The police . . . are not as — how can I say it? — not as suited for this job as others may be."

"The Silver Jaguar Society," Anna said proudly, as if she'd already solved the crime herself. And, José thought, as if she'd forgotten that the Silver Jaguar Society member standing in front of her had swiped the cup in the first place.

Alejandro nodded and glanced toward the door. "Ah . . . this is why I must ask you to go now," he said abruptly, pulling his hands from his pockets. The lump of money stayed buried as Alejandro led them out of the cultural center and toward the trail that went back to the lodge. "I must do what needs to be done to find the cup before it is lost to us forever."

A small green Volkswagen Bug pulled into the cultural center parking lot. Alejandro held up his finger, signaling the driver to wait, and turned back to the kids. "I hope that you do not think less of me," he said quickly, blinking hard. "I . . . I am going to make this right." He looked back at the convertible. The squatty bird-watcher who had hogged the dinner rolls was climbing out of the driver's seat.

"Hey, he's staying at the lodge," Sofia said.

"He is probably lost . . . looking for directions. You go on home; I'll see what he needs."

They started down the path, but then José turned. "Hey, Alejandro?" he called.

Alejandro paused. "Yeah?"

"When you went out before to talk with that . . . with whoever came earlier . . . were they looking for directions, too?"

"Ah, yes. . . . yes . . . happens often." He held up his hands to the sky and shook his head. Those constantly lost tourists . . . what could you do about them?

José nodded slowly. "Yeah . . . well, good luck with everything."

"*Gracias*, my friend." Alejandro walked up to the dinner-roll guy as José, Anna, Henry, and Sofia started back down the path.

"You guys —" Anna started to say, but Sofia held up a hand to stop her and hurried farther along the path. José understood right away what she was doing; she didn't want Alejandro to hear them talking.

Finally, Sofia stopped and turned to them. "Look. I know what you're going to say. He lied. He did. I don't know why. But I know Alejandro, and —"

"It doesn't matter how long you've known him," José interrupted. "He that first cries out 'stop thief' is often he that has stolen the treasure."

"Who are you quoting this time?" Henry asked.

"I don't know. Some English playwright." José waved at the air. "But the point is, Alejandro was the last one to see the real cup. And now he's claiming somebody stole it from him? We have to check this out."

"Dude. When did *you* turn into Sherlock Holmes?" Henry asked.

José was a little surprised at himself, too. But bits of conversation and images from the cultural center flashed through his head, arranging and rearranging themselves — the devil masks, the Russian woman, the cave, the money bulging in Alejandro's pocket, his shaky voice. And those bits arranged themselves into an answer whose pieces fit together in a way that the numbers in José's math problems never did.

The paper in his backpack didn't matter. It was okay that he couldn't use all his presidential quotes, and he didn't need to memorize any more words of wisdom from famous nature guys. He was figuring this out; he was going to save the Jaguar Cup the way they'd saved the flag. But this time, he'd take the lead.

He knew what to do, and he was already imagining himself having dinner with his parents when they made it back to the lodge, telling them all about how he figured it out.

"José?" Anna waved a hand in front of his day-dreaming face. "What are you thinking?"

"Remember what you said about the Jaguar Cup thief being *here* . . . and not in San José?"

Anna nodded.

"I think you were right about that," José said. "But you were wrong about something else. It's not Vincent Goosen." He swallowed hard and looked at Sofia. Being smart and right wasn't as easy as he thought it was going to be. But he had to say it; this was his chance to solve everything. "I think Alejandro is lying. I don't think anyone else stole that cup. At least not yet. And if we hurry, I think I know where we can find it."

NINE

"Are you sure *this* is the cave on the map he gave her?" José eyed the tiny entrance on the other side of the muddy stream. Coming here to follow the Russian woman through the cave to find the Jaguar Cup — it sure *sounded* like Alejandro had hidden it here, anyway — had seemed like such a good idea when he'd shared it back on the jungle trail. But that was the thing about sounding smart — people tended to nod and go along with you, even when you got there and what seemed like a brilliant plan turned scary, claustrophobic, and wet.

"This has to be it," Sofia said. "I told you. It's the only cave around here, other than the one down the road with the big signs for tours, and that one's open to the public. She wouldn't have needed directions or a map to find it. And besides . . . look." Sofia pointed down the dirt road, where the woman's Jeep was parked.

"So she's already in there." José took a deep breath.

"She's parked by the other entrance," Sofia said. "That's the easy route, but it's a lot longer. It'll be at least an hour before she's all the way in."

"So this cave's . . . not open to the public?" Henry asked, eyeing the tiny entrance. "It doesn't look like much of the public would fit. Is it safe?"

"It's not dangerous. It's off-limits because it's a sensitive ecosystem. Our ecotourism board and the guides have agreed not to bring tourists here." Sofia sighed. "That's why . . . well . . . I'm a little surprised Alejandro would send her here. It's against all the rules."

"Yeah, well, so is stealing artifacts when you're supposed to be packing them up for an exhibit," Henry said, and started slogging across the stream toward that tiny crevice in the rock.

"I still can't imagine . . ." Sofia began, but she stopped and sighed again. José felt kind of bad for her. It had to be hard finding out somebody close to you wasn't the person you thought.

"There is no way I'm fitting through here," Henry said, sticking an arm into the darkness of the crack.

"Yes you are," Sofia said. "My dad's been in here, and he's bigger than you." She sat down at the bottom of the crevice, where it was a little wider. "You go feet first here," she said, wiggling into the cave that way until only the top half of her body was sticking out. Then she flipped over onto her belly. "And then you can turn over and you should feel . . . there. There are footholds along the wall, and then you climb down to the floor." She sank into the dark until only her hands were left, and then they vanished, too.

"Sofia?" Anna peeked into the blackness.

"Okay!" Sofia called. "Now that I'm down, I can shine a light up so you can find the footholds easier. Who's next?"

Anna went next, then José and Henry, who lost his handhold and sort of fell the last few feet. He stumbled over José and landed in a puddle of muck. "Aw, man," Henry said, standing and wiping his hands on his pants. "I'm covered in mud."

"It's not mud," Sofia said. "It's guano."

"What-o?"

"Guano." She shined her flashlight at her face so Henry could see her smile. "Bat poop, Henry. Come on this way. And be quiet now. We should be able to catch up with her quickly."

She shined her light between two rock faces, slick with water and slime, and José followed her through the narrow passageway with Anna behind him, and Henry at the end of the line.

"Sofia, how big is this cave? I mean . . . it seems like . . ." José stopped. He hated the scared sound of his voice. It was pathetic, compared to the guy on the path back there, Mr. I-know-where-we-can-find-it. Here he was now with no clue where to find anything — not even the next place to put his foot in this dark mess, much less the Jaguar Cup. "Where are we going?" he finally asked.

"Stay there for a second," Sofia said quietly. "I'm going to climb up and then shine the light down so you can see where to put your hands and feet." She braced her legs against the rock walls and pulled herself up into an opening in the cave ceiling.

"There," José heard from over his head, and then the light shone down on what looked like a very smooth, foothold-free wall. "Come on up!" Sofia whispered.

It took him longer, but José made it up and found himself standing in a slightly bigger cave room. The sound of rushing water came from the other side, but Sofia's light didn't reach far enough to show where it was rushing.

"Can you hold this for them?" Sofia asked, and handed José the flashlight so he could illuminate Henry and Anna's path.

"What I was asking," José said — it was easier to talk when he knew she couldn't see him — "is where do you think we should look?"

"I thought *you* knew where to find it." Even in the dark, he couldn't miss the mocking in Sofia's whisper.

"I'm kidding. If it's here — and I still don't know about this, José — but *if* Alejandro hid the cup, if he hid *anything* here, there's only one place it would probably be, and that's the cathedral."

"The cathedral?" Anna said, brushing her hands off on her pants as Henry struggled up the chute below her.

"It's a ways up here," Sofia said. "You'll see."

Henry pulled himself up, panting.

"Everybody ready?" Sofia asked.

"Can't we take a break for a minute?" Henry huffed.

"With all the time you spend chasing pirates and robbers and performing secret missions, Henry, I thought you'd be in better shape," Sofia teased.

"His thumb muscles are super powerful," Anna said, laughing.

"Shhh. Come on." José couldn't join in the Henry-mocking. His stomach was all bunched up, and he wanted to get on with this. He needed to find the Jaguar Cup and get out of here and back to the lodge so his parents could come back and he'd be their awesome, smart, mystery-solving kid and everything would be great again. "We're never going to catch up with her if we don't keep moving."

"You're right." Sofia took the light back — it flickered, but she jiggled it and it came back on — and sloshed her way across the shallow water that puddled on the floor of this room. The rushing sound got louder.

"Waterfall," she said, shining the light into a deep crevice where water gushed down from higher than the light would show. Past the waterfall, Sofia squeezed into another crevice. This one kept going, and they sidled along until it opened up into a wider tunnel. Sofia climbed up and over some boulders that stuck out from the side of the cave and through another narrow passageway. José followed, listening for Anna's quick steps and Henry's thunking ones behind him.

"Duck low here," Sofia said, dropping down. "You're going to have to scootch along on your belly for a while."

José tried to imitate her, wiggling forward on his elbows until the belly-crawling tunnel started to get wider and a little taller, and there was noise coming from ahead. Another waterfall, maybe. But weird-sounding. Higher pitched.

"This is it," Sofia said quietly, almost reverently, crawling forward and climbing to her feet. "The cathedral." She shined the light back at the tunnel so Anna and Henry could see to climb out.

"Now listen for a second," Sofia said, clicking off the light.

The dark of this room was the darkest José had ever seen. Way darker than his room at home, where the streetlights shone through his blinds. Even darker than the lodge rooms at night, where either the moon or flashes of lightning always seemed to be visiting at the windows. This was pure-black, velvet-thick dark.

But it wasn't quiet.

The high-pitched waterfall sound was louder in this room. No . . . it wasn't like water, actually. More like a whistling wind. With . . . squeaks?

Sofia flipped the light back on and swept it slowly around the room.

"Wow," Anna whispered. "The cathedral. That's perfect." And for once, her notebook and pen stayed in her pocket. José understood. Some things were too wild and different for words, and this was one of them. The walls were lined with crystal formations that glowed and reflected in the shallow lake that covered the cave floor. Water cascaded down the glittering crystal columns in perfectly smooth sheets. The ceiling was a huge sand-colored dome, mottled with black and brown.

"Wait," Henry said, a wary edge in his voice. "Am I dizzy, or is that ceiling moving?"

Sofia took a step farther into the room, and a cloud of bats exploded into motion from the wall nearby, their wings whooshing and fluttering. Henry squeezed both hands into fists at his sides, and José could practically see the thought bubble bursting out of his head. *I will not run away. I will not run away.*

It was the most amazing place José had ever seen, but it wasn't why they were here. "Sofia, where did you think we might find . . . something hidden?"

She stepped up to the wall and shone her light into a crevice. Nothing but smooth stone. She moved along a couple feet and tried another one. Three bats swooped out at her indignantly. "The walls of this place are perfect hiding spots," she said. "In fact, it was a cave sort of like this one where they found the Jaguar Cup to begin with, so if Alejandro were going to hide it, then maybe . . ." She shone the light into another crevice and shook her head. "I wish we had another light. We'll have to go all the way around, and . . ." She paused and held a finger to her lips, then clicked off the light.

"Did you hear that?" she whispered.

José listened. Over the rush of the bats' wings and the squeaks of their echolocation searching for one another in the dark, were splashing footsteps, coming from the opposite side of the cathedral.

TEN

"We need to hide," José whispered. "Back in the tunnel!" Without the light, he couldn't see a thing, but he ran his hand along the cool, slippery rocks, shuffling his feet in the water, tapping against rock wall with his toes until he felt the opening. "Here," he whispered, and guided Sofia, Anna, and Henry back into the tunnel before he knelt and wiggled his way back on his belly, too. He stared into the blackness ahead and waited.

"Dude, watch your foot. That was my ear," Henry hissed.

"Can you still hear the splashing?" came Anna's voice from behind him. José listened. There was nothing. Then . . . yes! "It's getting closer. And there's a light. Shhh!"

The ghost of a light had fogged its way into the room. Now it was spreading, covering more of the walls with every splooshing step. José saw the flashlight itself poke out from what must have been one of the crevices on the other side. Then a long, thin arm. Then a leg and then the rest of the Russian woman from the cultural center. She said something — José had no idea what — to a tall man who was with her, and then started shining her light into crevices along the cave walls, just as Sofia had been doing.

"She's looking for it in the crevices," José whispered. "What if they find it?" His heart sank. What could they do? Wiggle out on their bellies with their tiny light and shout, "Hey, you guys! Give us that cup!" They were four kids, and nobody even knew they were here. There was nothing they could do — absolutely nothing.

"Ah!" the woman cried, shining her light into the wall, and the man sloshed his way over, and then they both were blabbing on and on in Russian.

"What's going on?" Anna hissed from behind him. But José's mouth was too dry to talk, his throat too tight and choked to answer.

"Dude, what *is* it?" Henry grabbed José's boot and gave it a good shake.

"They found it," José whispered. His voice was flat. He'd lost. He'd lost his only chance to fix everything —

and now all he could do was lean on his elbows in the soggy bat poop and watch them leave with the Jaguar Cup.

There was a flash. And then another flash.

"What are they doing?" Henry whispered.

"They're . . ." Neither the man nor the woman was making any move to get the cup. They were . . . "They're taking photographs."

He frowned and squinted, but he couldn't see into the crevice — the angle was wrong.

Henry jiggled his boot again. "What are they doing now?"

"They're . . . sort of standing there. Looking at it." José's elbows were aching. When were they going to take the thing and leave? If he and Anna and Henry and Sofia couldn't save the cup, at least they could maybe follow these people and then let someone know where they were.

"Now what are they doing?" Anna whispered.

"They're still standing there looking at it."

The man said something, and the woman said something back and sounded a little sad. And then he put his arm around her and they started walking. Wait . . . were they going to *leave* it there? That didn't make any sense at all. But they were. "They're leaving," José whispered.

Sure enough, the flashlight faded and the footprints splashed quieter and quieter until the thick black returned and even the bats settled down. José wiggled back into the open and waited for Sofia to come with the light. She shone it across the cathedral. "Where were they?"

José pointed a little to the left of where she was shining. "Right . . . there." He was almost afraid to hope. "So I guess we should . . . go look."

Anna shook her head. "They wouldn't have left it there. Are you sure they didn't take it when you weren't looking?"

"They didn't take anything," José said. "Maybe . . . maybe they're coming back for it."

"Why wouldn't they take it now?" Anna said.

"Because," Henry piped up. "The treasure is safest at the bottom of the sea!"

Sofia shone the light in his eyes. "What?"

He squinted and waved it away. "The treasure is safest at the bottom of the sea. That's what Mad Ben the Pirate always says. When you find the treasure, you leave it until you're ready to lift anchor because that way you don't get caught with the goods."

Anna sighed. "Henry, we're not dealing with pirates. Or video games."

But José's heart lifted. "But he's right. Maybe they left it because they're not ready to leave . . . like, maybe their flight isn't for a few more days, or maybe the roads are still a problem with the earthquake, or something. So they left it." He started sloshing across the big open room. "They left it right here so they can come back for it, only we're going to get to it first! Sofia, gimme that light, will you?" He reached behind him, waving frantically for the light and knocked it right out of her hands.

There was a splash. The light glowed, all murky in the brown-yellow guano-water of the pool for a second before it faded and went out.

The blackness of the cave felt like it was pressing on José's chest.

"Well, that didn't go well," Sofia said into the dark. "It's okay. That other passage — the long, easy route — has a lot more natural light. We need to feel our way over there. Let me just —" José heard some sloshing around in the water by their feet. "Got it," Sofia said. He heard the batteries rattling in the light as she shook it. But the dark stayed dark. "Shoot. It's totally dead."

"Here," Anna said, and José felt her hand creep down his arm to his hand. "Everybody grab a hand so we stay together. I'll put my other hand out in front of my face so we don't walk into any walls."

They baby-stepped their way across the cathedral, which seemed four times as wide as it had in the light, their rubber boots gurgling and slurping in the dark, until finally, Anna said, "There."

"Okay. The path out the long way is right here." Sofia tugged at José's other hand, pulling him off to the left, away from the spot where that crevice and the Jaguar Cup must have been.

José pulled back. "Wait," he said. "We can't leave it here. They're going to come back; I know they are." He felt certain again, smart. He needed to leave this place with what he came for. "Let me just . . ." He wiggled his hands away from Anna and Sofia and reached out in front of him, shuffling forward until his hand touched cool, wet rock. "They had only checked four, maybe five crevices before that lady started shouting . . ." He eased his hand into the first crevice and felt nothing but more cool rock. ". . . so it can't be too far from here . . ."

"José, I really don't think —"

"We *can't* just leave."

The second crevice was deeper. José felt along all of its edges. Nothing.

"José, this is silly," Sofia's voice called from the tunnel that would lead them out. But not yet, José thought. Not until he had that cup. He reached into the next crevice, and felt fur and then fluttering and then a rush of bat-wing wind whooshed past him. He sucked in his breath. He was not going to pull a Henry and go running away from things that couldn't hurt him. Not when he was this close. The next crevice would be the fifth one, and he thought that was probably about where they'd been.

This one was narrower and deeper. José stretched

his arm as far as it would go and felt his fingers graze something that wasn't rock and moved when he'd poked it. "You guys, hold on, I think . . ." He stretched his arm farther and extended his fingers. Had he pushed it out of reach? But no . . . there was something, and it . . .

"GAHHHHH-SOMETHING'S-CRAWLING-UP-MY-ARRRRRMMMMM!" José flung and flapped and twirled and whipped his arm back and forth until he lost his balance completely and splashed, face-first into the water, out of breath.

Then Sofia's light came on. "Oh good! It's back," she said, shining it on José's sogginess. She stepped up to the crevice where he'd been reaching and reaching, shone the light inside, and smiled. She reached in and pulled out a gigantic, gangly spider by the tip of one long, skinny leg. It looked like some superhero daddy longlegs. "There's a whole nest of them in here."

"Holy alien arachnids," said Henry, stepping back. "Dude, I am so glad that thing wasn't crawling up me."

Sofia held it out to José. "Here's your treasure," she said. "It's a tailless whip scorpion. Otherwise known as 'that ginormous cave spider' that the tourists will pay big money to see." She gently eased the scorpion-spider thing back into the crevice and reached down to help José to his feet.

"Now can we leave?"

He nodded.

"Well," Henry said, sloshing his way into the tunnel. Columns of light spilled in from above them now. "That explains why the Russian lady didn't want to take it home with her. Got any more ideas for where the cup might be?"

José didn't answer. He didn't have any more ideas, and even if he had, they probably would have been as dumb as this one.

ELEVEN

The hike out of the cave the "easy way" took them two hours, and by the time they pulled themselves up a narrow chute that Sofia called the chimney, José's stomach was grumbling for food.

"Hurry up, Henry," he said, standing at the edge of the dirt road where they'd seen the Russian lady's car before. She and her husband were long gone, probably already showing off their pictures of the monster cave spiders. "Come on, I'm hungry."

Sofia pulled some granola bars out of her backpack and handed them out. "It's not the greatest lunch, but it's better than nothing."

Two mountain bike riders sped past, splashing up mud. José didn't even bother to get out of the way. Why did it matter? In a few hours, he'd gone from being the smart kid again to the dumbest kid ever.

Once you'd led your friends on a wild-goose chase that ended with you splashing around in a big old bat-poop puddle, well, you didn't really have to worry much about the day getting worse.

Another three mountain bikers came speeding down the hill, spraying José with more mud-puddle specks.

"You okay?" Sofia asked him.

"I'm fine," he said, wiping mud from his face with his sleeve as Henry climbed the rest of the way out of the cave.

"What's with the bikers?" Anna asked Sofia as they started walking along the road, eating their warm granola bars. "They've all got numbers on their backs."

"It's the Adventure Race," Sofia said. "Three days of biking, zip lining, white-water kayaking, and trekking through the mountains and rain forest. Dad was so excited when he saw the route. A bunch of them will be at the lodge later, once they finish."

They walked along the road, ducking to the sides when more bikers sped past. Close to the lodge, they discovered a bunch of bikes parked at the racers' destination: RAGING RIVER ZIP LINE TOURS.

"Oh, let's go watch!" Sofia said "Dad told me they were doing the course here."

Anna, Henry, and José followed her through the maze of parked mountain bikes and up a gravel driveway to an open field. Exhausted bikers were sprawled all over the place, lying on the ground. José wondered if anyone had warned them about those biting ants.

Other cyclists, still in their helmets, climbed a steep, rickety flight of stairs up to the top, where they strapped themselves into harnesses. The first man in line reached up, clipped his harness to a cable that stretched out from the top of the tower and disappeared into a hole cut in the trees. "*¡Adiós, amigos!*" he called, grabbed onto the harness straps, and launched himself off the platform. The zip line made a whirring, whining hum as he flew away from them and disappeared into the open space in the trees.

Henry's mouth hung open. "Dude . . . it looks like the forest ate that guy."

José's stomach felt like it was dropping off that platform, too. The whole idea of letting go like that . . . he shivered. He didn't even like those big swings at the amusement park. Flying seemed like a terrible idea unless you were a bird. *Keep your eyes on the stars and keep your feet on the ground*, Theodore Roosevelt had said. He probably meant it figuratively, but José was happy to adapt the quote to his anti-amusement-park-ride philosophy.

Sofia laughed at Henry, still standing with his mouth gaping open. "Don't worry. He'll come out at the next platform. Then he's got seven more lines to go. The course crosses the river twice and ends up back here." She pointed to a distant hill. "That's the highest one, over the ravine. It's pretty amazing."

"Yeah. Sounds it." José said, nodding. If he wasn't going to be smart, he could at least pretend to be brave. And that was easy when all you had to do was watch the muddy adventure guys do the launching and whizzing and getting eaten by trees.

"You think so?" Sofia's face lit up. "Because the fifth line actually passes right by our lodge and I know Liza who runs this place, and she'll totally let us use it as a shortcut back if you want. I do it all the time. I know you're hungry, and it'll save us like half an hour."

"Umm . . ." José wasn't hungry anymore. He thought fast, then leaned in and whispered to Sofia. "I don't think Henry's up for that, and we should probably stay together, you know . . . just in case."

Thankfully, she didn't ask him just in case what, so they headed back to the road and started walking again. After about twenty minutes, Sofia veered onto a path through the forest. "Come on. This path connects with the lodge trails. It'll spit us out near the bridge, behind the pool."

In a few minutes, the turns of the trails felt more familiar, and José spotted the bridge, still all high and bouncy looking. "Hey!" he said, squinting into the setting sun on the other side. "Somebody's coming across from the primary forest. Were there tours this afternoon?"

Sofia shrugged. "Maybe. A bunch of local guides take tourists on walks over there." She raised her hand to shade her eyes and frowned. "That's Alejandro — and that guy from the cultural center — the one he thought was asking for directions."

Anna tipped her head thoughtfully. "I wonder why he hired Alejandro. Doesn't your dad take lodge guests to the primary forest all the time?"

Sofia watched them crossing the bridge and frowned. "He probably wanted to see something that's not on Dad's tour."

"Like what?" Henry asked. "Ha! Look at that guy; he's holding those railings so hard his knuckles must be white." The dinner-roll guy didn't seem to like the bouncing and wobbling any more than José and Henry did.

"Like the cave with the spiders?" José asked.

Sofia nodded. "Maybe. Dad and Alejandro don't always see eye to eye. The ecotourism board sets some sites that are off-limits for tours — sometimes because traffic can cause damaging erosion, sometimes because it can introduce diseases to sensitive habitats, like that cave, sometimes because turtles or birds are nesting, and sometimes because the animals there are endangered and too vulnerable."

"And Alejandro doesn't worry about that?" Anna said.

"It's not that he doesn't care," she said, "but if you can take a photographer to get a shot no one else will have or hand a lifelong bird-watcher a species she's never seen before . . ." She shrugged.

". . . you get paid a big wad of cash," José finished. Like the one in Alejandro's pocket. It was probably even fatter now, with whatever the dinner-roll guy had paid to get taken wherever he'd just been.

"But how can Alejandro do that?" Anna watched them crossing the bridge. "Can't the Silver Jaguar Society do something about it? I mean . . . he's taken an oath, hasn't he? To protect —"

"To protect the world's artifacts," Sofia said, turning to Anna. "And he's devoted his whole life to that." She turned to José. "Including the Jaguar Cup. But he's also got to eat and have someplace to sleep, and those things cost money, and in case you haven't noticed, there aren't exactly a million ways to make a living here unless you're giving tours to people like you. And him." She gestured toward the bridge, where the men were stepping off on this side.

"So . . . where do you think he took that guy?" José asked quietly.

They watched as Alejandro waved and started back over the bridge to go home. The man waved back and headed away from them, toward the reception area. His boots were caked to the knees with slimy, reddish mud.

"The Almendro Trail," Sofia said quietly, and started for the bridge. "Come on. It's not far at all. As long as everybody's breaking rules today, you might as well see, too."

TWELVE

Sofia took them over the bridge, up a hill, and along a trail that zigzagged through the forest. The path ended at the biggest tree José had seen since arriving in Costa Rica. It was all lumpy and gnarled, with vines hanging along its trunk. It wasn't quite as big as the redwoods José had seen visiting his uncle in California one time, but it was old. Wise-looking. José stepped right up to its trunk; being close to a tree like that couldn't help but make you a little smarter.

Sofia looked up into the high leaves, listening. "I can't tell if they're here."

Before José could ask who "they" were, a call floated over the forest behind them — *RAAHHH-RAH-AHHH* — and Sofia's face brightened. "This is perfect!" she whispered, pointing toward the treetops at the other side of the clearing. "The parents are coming. Be really still, and watch, right . . ." She paused, and there was a louder call — *RAAHHH!* — as two enormous green birds swooped over the treetops on powerful wings and landed on a thick branch that stuck out from the almendro tree above them.

"Oh, they're gorgeous!" Anna whispered. "What are they?"

Sofia beamed with pride as if they were her pets. "Great green macaws."

"They're pretty cool." Henry plopped himself down on a fallen log near the tree and stretched out his legs. Sofia sat on another log, pulled her sketchbook from her pocket, and started to draw, looking up, then down, then up.

José stared up at the birds. Their wingspans had to be five or six feet, and now that they'd landed, José could see not only the green-yellow-blue of their wings but also a fluff of bright red feathers around their sharp, curved beaks.

"There used to be huge flocks of them here," Sofia said, staring up at the branch. "But with all the logging the past twenty years or so, they're more and more threatened. They're starting to come back, so they've become a symbol of the conservation movement. To lose even one nest right now would be awful. That's why we're not supposed to lead tours out here."

"But *looking* at the birds won't hurt them, will it?" Anna said.

"No. But some people do more than look. These birds — if you capture babies — are worth a lot on the black market. We keep a pretty good eye on the almendro tree across from the lodge, but this tree's so far out that nobody's watching over it most of the time. It's safer to keep the location under wraps."

"Where's the actual nest?" José asked.

As if it had heard him, one of the birds ruffled its feathers, then climbed along the branch and underneath it to a hole in the tree trunk. "That's where another branch broke off, a long time ago," Sofia said. "Makes a perfect nesting hole."

They watched as the second bird picked its way around the hole and disappeared inside. "Must be lunch time for the babies," Sofia said quietly, stepping back to try and get a better view. "Oh, you guys, come here. You haven't seen leaf cutter ants yet, have you?"

"Only on our school trip to the Biodome in Montreal," Anna said.

Sofia pointed down at a long line of . . . walking leaves? No . . . there were ants under the leaves. But the ants were tiny compared to the bright green loads they carried. José knelt to get a better look, then stood and jumped back. "Do these sting or bite or kill you or anything?"

Sofia laughed. "No, they're too busy collecting leaves."

"For food?" José was mesmerized by the never-ending parade. Ants hauling leaves on their backs marched in one direction, while empty-handed ants went the other way.

"No, they eat fungus that they grow in underground gardens. They chew up the leaves and use them as kind of a fertilizer for the fungus. A colony this size could strip the leaves off a whole tree in one day."

"Whoa." Henry squatted, staring at the ants. "That's serious damage for such little dudes."

Sofia shrugged. "There's power in numbers."

José walked along the line of ants to see if he could spot the tree where they were getting the leaves. But the ants marched past the almendro tree into the distance and kept going. On the other side of the almendro tree, José looked up again, into a big, dark opening in the bark.

"There's another hole in the tree over here!" he called. It was a perfect hiding place.

"Yep," Sofia said, joining him at the far side of the tree. "It's hollow pretty much right up to the top. You can climb right in there if you want."

José stepped over the tangle of roots at the base of the tree. His heart sped up. He didn't want to say it aloud, but what if this was where Alejandro had hidden the cup? What if he was working with the dinner-roll guy and not that Russian lady? They didn't look like they'd been carrying anything big when they came over the bridge. What if the Jaguar Cup was right here?

José had to turn sideways to slip into the dark of the tree. It was almost as black as the cave, and there were high-pitched peeps coming from above him. Baby macaws? He felt a drip in his hair, then another one, and looked up. Could it have started raining a little? Michael said the clouds would move in and start rumbling and pouring pretty much every afternoon while they were here. A few more drops landed on his cheeks. At least it was a warm rain.

José could hear Henry outside the tree grumbling about food and knew he'd need to hurry. Could the inside of this trunk have little crevices and shelves like the cave? He ran his hand along the inside curve of the tree. It was rough and splintery-damp, but soft in some spots, too. Moss, maybe. Anything could grow in here in the moisture. There was no place to hide a golden cup, though. José dropped down to his knees and felt around the base, just to be sure, but it was all moss and mud.

Stupid. There was no cup here. José turned sideways and eased himself back into the dappled light of the forest, glad he hadn't said anything about his dumb idea this time. At least he'd come out of the tree in better shape than he'd emerged from that dumb spider cave.

Except — he looked up at the sunlight flickering in the canopy leaves — it wasn't raining. At all.

Sofia frowned at him and reached up to wipe at his cheek with her sleeve. "You've got some bat poop on your face," she said, smiling. "Come on. Let's get some food."

By the time they reached the river, real rain was pounding the leaf canopy overhead. The hanging bridge was slippery with mud from their boots, and José was relieved when he stepped off on the lodge side of the river. His stomach ached for food. It was after six, and that granola bar hadn't been much of a lunch.

Henry was obviously feeling the same way. "Can we go straight to dinner, or do we need to clean up first?"

"Hmm." Sofia looked them over. "The rain actually washed off a lot of the mud and guano, so I think we're okay." She started for the dining hall. "Besides, lots of people go right to the dining room from hiking."

They were passing the swimming pool when Carlos, one of the lodge maintenance workers, came rushing down the path. "Sofia, your dad needs to see you in the reception area. Pronto. Where have you been?"

"Out hiking." She hurried along behind him and didn't bother changing out of her mud-covered boots as she rushed up to the reception desk. José, Henry, and Anna waited at the entrance, but Michael waved them to come in.

"Your parents are on the phone." He handed the phone to José.

"Mom? Dad?" José's voice broke. He pressed the phone to his cheek and turned away from the others. He had so wanted to solve the mystery of the cup, but now . . . now he just wanted his parents to come so they could all go home. "How's it going? Are you on your way to the lodge?"

"It's going okay." It was his mom. "We miss you, buddy. The roads are open again, but our rental car died this afternoon as we were about to set out. Michael's going to come pick us up."

"Okay. Any progress with the cup?"

"Well . . . you know that Alejandro doesn't have it, right?"

"Well . . . yeah, I guess."

"We have some new concerns," his mom said. "Virtually no one knew when and how that . . . item was to be transported, so unless it was an inside job by one of the other Gold Museum staff members, which we doubt, then it had to be someone exceptionally well connected. Someone — or a *group* of someones — who's pulled off this kind of heist before."

"The Serpentine Princes?" José whispered into the phone. Geez, could Anna be right, wondering if Vincent Goosen was hanging around hiding behind some tree?

"Possibly," his mom said quietly. "That's what we've been working on." She sounded tired.

"Your voice is all scratchy," José said.

"I've been on the phone all day. We haven't had Internet access here since the earthquake, and even the phone connections are still sketchy. We just finished making calls to confirm the whereabouts of all fifteen known members of that . . . organization you asked about."

"And . . . ?" José looked at Anna out of the corner of his eye — she was going to flip when she heard this — and felt a twinge of resentment. How come some people's ideas always ended up being right while other people ended up covered in bat poop?

"They're all confirmed at home in Europe," his mom said.

"Good."

"Except one."

"Which one?" José asked.

"The . . . ah . . . the big one." She didn't say his name. She didn't have to. It was Vincent Goosen. The ringleader. "But that doesn't mean anything, really. He could be anywhere, though it does . . . well . . . concern us."

It concerned José, too. What if Anna was right? What if Goosen was here? He was a whole lot scarier than Alejandro.

"Actually, there were two possible suspects we couldn't pin down, but the other one isn't a member of the group any longer. Still . . . I'd like you guys to be mindful of . . . what?" José could hear another woman — maybe Anna's mom? — saying something in the background. "Okay . . . yes, you're probably right," his mom said, all muffled, and then spoke back into the phone. "Sorry about that. Anyway, we have to go now. Please tell Anna her mom says hello and she loves her and to be good."

"Okay, I love you."

"Love you, too, sweetie. See you soon."

He handed the phone back to Sofia's dad. Anna frowned.

"Sorry." José shrugged. "They had to go. I'm supposed to tell you your mom loves you and be good."

Anna rolled her eyes, but not before José saw them get a little watery.

"Listen, kids." Michael turned to them, his face serious. "José, I'm sure your mom told you they've got car troubles. I'm going to drive the Jeep to pick them up."

"Will you be back tonight?" Sofia asked.

Michael shook his head. "The roads are still in rough shape, so I won't get there until late. We should be back by noon tomorrow." He gestured to a young woman working at the computer behind the desk. "Luci's offered to be on call if the four of you need anything while I'm gone, okay?"

Luci looked up from updating the lodge's nature blog long enough to give a quick wave.

"No problem." Sofia reached up to give her dad a hug. "We'll just hang out around the lodge tonight." She glanced at Henry, settled on a wicker chair, staring vacantly up at the lodge television. "Somebody's not used to exercise that involves more than his thumbs."

They went to the dining room and managed to convince the serving ladies to get them some rice and beans, even though official dinner hours were over. Nobody said much.

Henry shoveled food in his face as fast as possible.

Anna and Sofia kept handing their notebooks back and forth — Anna's news notes and Sofia's drawings. Sofia kept glancing up at José, then down at the notebook, scribbling. Were they passing notes about him?

"Hey, can I see your sketches of the green macaws?" José asked her, reaching for the sketchbook.

Sofia pulled it toward her and made eye contact with Anna, biting her lip. "I'm . . . not done with it, so no."

"You showed *her*," José said.

Sofia shot another look at Anna — the kind of look you give somebody who knows a secret you're not telling the other person who's sitting there with a plateful of lukewarm rice and beans and no appetite anymore. The kind of look you give one person when you've been laughing at the other person who doesn't know the secret and who spent the whole day making up dumb ideas.

"I get it," José said.

Sofia put her notebook in her pocket. "Maybe later, okay?"

"Fine." José stood up, dumped his food in the garbage, put his plate in the dirty dishes rack, and turned to Henry, who had shoved a last bite of cornbread into his mouth. "You done?"

Something that sounded like "Mrrrful" came out of Henry's mouth, along with a spray of cornbread crumbs, but he got up and followed José down the steps and along the walkway back to their room.

José sank down on his bed. "When I was on the phone with my mom, she said they've been trying to track down any possible suspects," he started to tell Henry, but Henry was focused on opening the safe.

"Henry, are you even listening?"

"Huh?" He looked up quickly and slammed it shut again.

"What's in there?" José asked.

"Nothing," said Henry, flopping back onto the bed and turning on his GamePrism. "My passport and stuff. Man, I am wiped out." He leaned back against his pillow and started poking at game buttons. Even being wiped out, Henry's thumbs were still going strong.

José watched him for a minute. What could Henry have in that safe that he didn't want seen? Between the safe-door-slamming and notebook-slamming, it felt as if everybody was keeping secrets.

Well, fine, José thought, pulling the fifth Harry Potter book from his backpack. He was glad Henry hadn't bothered listening when he tried to tell him about the Serpentine Princes.

José could keep a secret of his own.

THIRTEEN

Henry was snoring, his GamePrism still in his hands, lighting his face with a greenish glow. But José couldn't sleep. He was glad his parents were coming back in the morning, but the thought of that envelope in his backpack pricked at his insides. He was going to have to tell them sometime.

He'd been reading Harry Potter by flashlight, but his batteries were starting to get all wimpy and weak. He clicked off the light, put his book down, flopped onto his back, and started writing a new story in his head.

Once upon a time, there was a golden Jaguar Cup, a symbol for the people who had saved it from Spanish invaders. Those same people had saved countless artifacts as gifts to the world.

Once upon a time, a man wanted to save that golden cup again. He wanted to hide it and keep it safe, but before he could, another man stole it away.

José squeezed his eyes shut. He needed to see the face of that shadowy figure in the story. But the thief disappeared into an alleyway while a security guard stood nearby.

Wait.

José paused at the bottom of his imaginary page. Alejandro had said there was a security guard at the Gold Museum. Why didn't the guard help Alejandro? Why didn't he save the Jaguar Cup? Wasn't that what security guards were for?

José started over.

Once upon a time, there was a man who wanted to steal a priceless artifact, so he disguised himself as a museum security guard and waited outside on the night the artifact was to be moved.

Could that be it? Could it be that the security guard didn't try to stop Goosen because the security guard *was* Goosen?

Lightning flashed, and José jolted upright in his bed. His heart pounded underneath his T-shirt. For a second, he thought about waking Henry, but then lightning flashed again and lit up the safe, and José remembered that Henry was a secret-keeping jerk and probably wouldn't wake up to listen anyway.

But he had to tell *somebody*.

Alejandro?

No.

José believed Alejandro's story now, but Alejandro was far away on the other side of a dark forest, and he certainly wasn't going to wake up Sofia because then he'd have to tell her and Anna, and they'd probably think he was being stupid.

And what if he was? He didn't want to end up all falling down wrong again. Not when they were already laughing at him over their notebook secrets.

He couldn't tell anybody until he was sure, and he needed more information.

José's parents hadn't been able to do research online because the earthquake knocked out their Internet in San José, but that shouldn't affect the Internet here at the lodge, right? In fact, that college-age girl who was supposed to be in charge of them now, the one from the front desk, had been working on the lodge's nature blog. She'd need Internet access to do that.

José slipped out of bed, slid his feet into his sneakers, and crept to the door. He couldn't get his thumping heart to settle down, and he didn't know why. Michael hadn't given them a curfew or anything, and if anyone asked, he could say he was thirsty and came over to fill his water bottle at the cooler in the reception area.

José grabbed his water bottle and opened the door to the dark, wet night. The thunder and lightning had moved on, but the rain still poured down in steady, silver sheets, like waterfalls spilling from the roofs of the rooms and walkways.

He hurried along the trail and up the ramp that led to the reception area, where he paused, listening. A steady rush of rain gushed behind him, but there were no guests checking in or even the usual TV noise from the desk. Good.

He took a deep breath and walked right into the reception room, past the desk without even looking — he was only here for water, after all — and only after he'd started filling his bottle did he turn to look casually back at the reception desk.

Empty.

And the computer behind it had been left on.

Perfect, José thought, screwing the lid back on his water bottle as he darted behind the desk. He could do his research, and if Luci came back, he'd act surprised that this wasn't a guest computer.

José sat down and typed Vincent Goosen's name into the search box, and a bunch of old news articles came up. It wasn't only the Silver Jaguar Society that was after Goosen — with more than two dozen suspected art thefts to his name, the gang leader was wanted by just about every law enforcement agency in the world. José scrolled through the search results. The most recent headline was from a couple months ago.

BREAK-IN ATTEMPT AT THE LOUVRE:
IS VINCENT GOOSEN BACK?

The articles before that were about Goosen's years of hiding after a record-breaking art theft. José skimmed one of the stories. He already knew that Goosen was suspected in a long list of unsolved heists dating all the way back to 1972, when he first betrayed the Silver Jaguar Society. The society had given Goosen a surveillance job at the Montreal Museum of Fine Arts, where curators worried that a skylight being repaired and other construction work had compromised the usual security.

They were right about that.

But they chose the wrong man for the surveillance job.

A few weeks after Goosen was sent to the museum in Montreal, armed thieves broke into the museum through that skylight with the disabled alarm. Authorities were sure Goosen had accomplices because he was notoriously afraid of heights — you'd never find him on a rooftop. Whoever those accomplices were, they lowered ropes, climbed down, bound and gagged the security guards on duty, and helped Goosen make off with millions of dollars in jewelry, figurines, and paintings. Members of the Silver Jaguar Society were devastated; Goosen was one of their best men. How could this have happened under his watch? They were embarrassed and horrified, and they wanted answers.

But Goosen had disappeared.

Since then, he'd been little more than a wealthy, eccentric shadow whose looping journeys around the world — Ireland, France, Sweden, America — could be traced only by the wake of stolen art left in his path. The rumors these days had Goosen holed up anywhere from a castle in Germany to a ski villa in the French Alps to some run-down apartment above a tattoo parlor in Amsterdam.

There was only one solid picture of him in all those years — a mug shot after police nabbed him leaving a museum in Austria twenty years ago. Goosen escaped the next day, and since then, there had been only a handful of hazy, maybe-it's-him-maybe-it's-not photos snapped in Paris bistros and Monte Carlo casinos.

José clicked on one of those — they were so blurry they reminded him of the pictures people said they took of Bigfoot and Champ, the Lake Champlain monster back home. The man with the wine glass in his hand wore a fedora that left most of his face in shadow. But he was laughing — José could see that — and he could just make out the tail of the snake tattoo curling above the man's collar. The symbol of the Serpentine Princes.

José scrolled through the article list again and sighed. None of this was current information, and it had nothing to do with where Goosen was now.

He tapped his fingers on the keyboard, stared out into the dark, and tried to replay the short conversation he'd had with his mom. They'd confirmed the whereabouts of all fifteen known Serpentine Prince members except Goosen. And wait . . . there was one other possible suspect, his mom said, who wasn't a member anymore. José frowned. She hadn't seemed interested in that other guy, but what if she should have been?

He turned back to the computer and clicked in the search box but didn't know what to type. "Guy who used to be a member of Serpentine Prince gang but isn't anymore?" His school librarian back home would shake her head at that pathetic search attempt. He settled on "Serpentine Prince members" and waited for the results to load.

The first result was a London newspaper article from two years ago that listed fifteen members, including Goosen. So . . . if one left . . . maybe there were sixteen before that? He scrolled down, looking for an older article with a similar list and was about to click on a 1990 story in the *Boston Globe* when a delicate bell tinged behind him.

José jumped about a foot off his chair, then whirled around to see a tall, wiry man leaning on the counter chuckling.

"Sorry to have given you a fright," the man said, "but I was hoping to check in."

FOURTEEN

"I . . . uh . . ." José turned back to the computer and closed the web browser — he didn't think the man could see what he'd been reading from the counter, but he didn't want to take any chances. "Actually, uh . . ." José faced the man again. "I'm not in charge."

"Really." The man's black mustache twitched as he tried not to smile. "You looked like you were working so diligently there. Must have been an interesting article."

"Can I help you, sir?" Luci came rushing in from the path that led to the rooms. "I am so sorry you had to wait. I had a guest who insisted she couldn't sleep with a lizard in her room." She rolled her eyes, then remembered the man was checking in. "Not that we have lizards in the rooms often, of course."

"Of course." The man smiled. "Lizards couldn't keep me awake tonight. I've had a long journey in the dark, and I'd like to check in. And get some dinner, if it's not too late."

"Sure." Luci rushed behind the counter and stopped short when she saw José at the computer.

"Sorry, I . . . uh . . ." José got up and motioned for her to take it. "Here."

Luci gave him a what-are-you-doing-here look, then asked the man at the desk, "May I have your name?"

"Gustave Millet."

Millet, José thought. José didn't know the name, but there was something about that guy. . . .

"Are you from France?" Luci asked, typing.

"I am from all over," the man said, chuckling again. He wore a zipped-up rain jacket over a tan shirt, with a black silk scarf knotted at his neck.

José couldn't stop staring. Something about this man felt familiar. Especially when he laughed.

José glanced back at the computer screen — no, that was dumb. Deciding that Vincent Goosen might show up simply because José had been reading about him was something Anna would do. But still . . . José couldn't keep himself from comparing this lodge guest to his memory of Goosen's photo. Goosen was older, though. His hair was gray. And he had more of it than this guy.

José wished the man would take off that scarf so he could check his neck for the tattoo.

"Here we go, sir." Luci printed out the man's room assignment and handed it to him, along with a key and a map. "You're going to follow this walkway." She traced the path with her finger. "You're in a garden room by the pool."

"Perfect." The man picked up his suitcase and asked Luci, "Where might I find a meal before I turn in?"

"Oh." She bit her lip. "Dinner's been over for hours, but I can have Isabelle make a sandwich for you. Give her a few minutes — maybe drop off your bags and then take a walk to the dining room?"

"I can show him where the rooms are if you want," José blurted out. The logical part of his brain was pretty sure this couldn't be Goosen, but some other part — probably the same brilliant part that messed up math problems and led him into the bat-poop cave — was working on a plan to find out.

Luci turned to him, as if she'd suddenly remembered finding him at her computer. "It's after midnight. What are you even doing awake?"

"Umm . . ." He spotted his water bottle by the computer. "I was getting a drink," he said. She raised her eyebrows.

"And then I saw the computer and figured I'd check my email while I was up."

"That's not a guest computer, you know," Luci said, handing him the water bottle.

"Oh," José said. "Sorry about that. So you want me to show Mr. . . . ah . . ."

"Millet," the man said. "I'd appreciate a guide, young man. Thank you."

"Sounds good," Luci said, already heading back to her computer. "And then go back to bed," she called over her shoulder to José. "You shouldn't be wandering all over at night."

"This area is quite . . . remote and wild, yes?" the man said, wheeling his suitcase along the path next to José. Rain cascaded down the roof in waterfalls on either side of the covered walkway.

"Yeah," José answered, wondering how he could get the man talking. "When the rain stops, you can see lots of animals. Birds, especially. Are you a bird-watcher?" He wondered if the man would say why he'd come.

"No, I'm more interested in art," the man said, and José's heart jumped into his throat so fast it nearly choked him.

"Like . . . uh . . . collecting it?" José stammered. But he didn't want to hear the answer. What was he *thinking*? Tromping off into the rain forest in the middle of the night with this man who could be the world's most —

"No. Creating it. I'm a painter."

"Oh." José laughed weakly. There he'd gone again, jumping to dumb conclusions like Anna.

"I'm hoping to work on some landscapes here," the man said, pausing where the path split off to the pool.

"It's this way." José pointed.

"And then I'm heading on to Tortuguero, to paint the village there."

"Neat," José said. He wanted to show this guy his room now and go back to bed. "It's right up here by the pool." José pointed to the small building near that tree where the sloth hung out. Rain poured off the edges of its thatched roof, and underneath, four doors led to the rooms.

"Thank you. I will find my way from here." The man turned to José and smiled — and there it was again. Something familiar. His mustache looked a little like the one José's seventh-grade social studies teacher had before he lost that Super Bowl bet and had to shave it off. But was it more than that? "One more thing?" the man asked. "The dining room?"

"Oh . . . right around the corner." José pointed, then headed in the opposite direction, back to his room. But after a few steps, he felt all twitchy again. He wasn't going to be able to sleep. He might as well find out for sure how stupid he was being.

José waited for the man's room door to close, then crept up to the small building. One room had a light on. José ducked low under its window and squatted in the leaf litter. The rain plastered his hair and soaked his clothes in a few seconds. There was no cover here.

His heart pounded. There was no glass in the window, and even over the rain, he could hear every move the man made inside.

Footsteps. Stopping.

Thump. A bag landing on the bed.

A long zipper. Was he taking off his jacket?

Slowly, José set down his water bottle and rose to peek in a corner of the window.

No. The man had unzipped his suitcase on the bed. He rummaged through clothes, pulled out a wooden box — maybe paints and brushes? — a pair of hiking boots, a cell phone charger, and a three-ring binder. Sweat dripped from José's forehead. It was so hot, so muggy — how could that guy still be wearing his jacket and scarf?

The man turned to the window — José ducked just in time.

Footsteps again.

Another zipper sound. José could barely control his breathing. Rain dripped from his hair into his eyes, but he swiped it away with a wet sleeve and crept up to peer in the window again.

The man was facing away from José, peeling off his rain jacket. He draped it over the desk chair, then unknotted his scarf. When he turned around to toss it on the bed, José sucked in his breath.

Curving around the strong muscles of the man's neck was the serpent tattoo.

Just as his jacket landed on the bed with a *phoof*, the man's eyes rose to the window.

José ducked.

But not in time.

FIFTEEN

At first, all José could hear was the rain and his own tripping footsteps as he crashed through the brush. There was no walkway on the side of the lodge where he'd crouched to spy on the man with the serpent tattoo — was it really Goosen? — so every step meant splashing through mud, fighting with roots and rotten tree stumps to stay on his feet.

The sharp tip of a branch caught José right under his eye. He slowed and put a hand to his stinging cheek — long enough to hear another pair of boots crunching through the forest underbrush. Whoever it was — it *had* to be Goosen, didn't it? Would a random guest who saw a kid peeping in through his window really take off chasing him through the jungle?

José ran. He made the most of the few open spaces between trees and vines to pick up time lost scrambling over saplings and logs. The rain let up a little. Sweat poured down his face, and his lungs ached. He couldn't hear anything over his own breathing and stumbling and tripping, but he knew the man would be on top of him if he paused even a split second to listen.

He didn't stop until a snarl of roots dug into his ankle with hard, wooden fingers and sent him flying onto his chest. In the moment he landed, he heard three things — heavy footsteps getting closer, a whoosh of air leaving his lungs, and — José fought for breath as he tried to stand. He whirled to his right. *There!* It was coming from over there — the muffled rush of the river.

José threw himself in the direction of the sound, and the scant moonlight bleeding through the trees grew stronger. He pushed on, flailing his arms in front of him to catch branches before they tore at his face, and finally burst onto one of the lodge's main trails.

He paused for a heartbeat — two, three — was this the trail that went back to his room off to the left? If it was, then turning right should lead him to the reception desk, where Luci could call for security if Goosen dared to follow him that far. But if he wasn't where —

The crack of a nearby branch breaking interrupted José's thoughts and sent him running — faster, so much faster without the roots and brambles to trip over — off to the right.

Behind him, the crack and scramble of forest running turned to a fast, steady thump of boots on concrete. The man shouted, "Stop right there!" in a sharp, hoarse roar — nothing like the voice of the smooth-talking guest back at the reception desk.

José ran, taking in great gulps of wet forest dark, willing his legs to move faster. He felt like he could drown in this thick, heavy air, but the footsteps behind him didn't yield and he pumped his arms as he pushed faster, faster as the trail curved to the left.

Keep moving! He pushed himself, running faster, faster, and the steady whoosh of the river grew to a roar.

Wait! No! He thought.

It was the wrong way!

The trail to the reception area led through the forest *away* from the river. This wasn't the sound of the gentle stream that wandered along the path closer to the rooms. So it had to be —

But he couldn't stop — not with the man so close behind him. Not even when the trail opened up to reveal the bridge. The swinging, swaying, bouncing bridge a million miles above the churning river. The stomach-twisting bridge that led into the total dark of the old-growth rain forest on the other side.

José wanted to stop and be sick, but he forced himself to keep running along the path that would soon turn into a thin-latticed layer of iron and air beneath his feet. *Courage is the power of the mind to overcome fear,* he told himself. That quote from Martin Luther King was one of his favorites, but it didn't seem to make his mind any more powerful right then.

Why did it have to be this path? Maybe he could still loop off onto one that led somewhere else. But when José risked slowing down for a frantic glance over his shoulder, the man was still there, still running strong. There was no way for José to turn back, no way for him to duck into the trees without getting all tangled and caught. He had to keep going, and there was only one place to go.

So when his feet pounded the last two steps of solid earth before the bridge began, José took one last, deep, shuddering breath and kept running.

Not even a quarter of the way across, he knew he'd made a mistake.

The bridge had swayed in a sickening enough arc with Sofia's teasing jumps. Now, it bucked violently under the pounding of José's thumping run, like a skinny metal horse desperate to throw him off.

José couldn't go on. He had to stop before his feet flew out from under him. He clung to the meager side rails and squeezed his eyes closed, listening for the man's footsteps, his heavy breathing, his sharp barking voice. José sucked in a shuddery breath and waited for that thick hand to close around his arm.

But it didn't.

And when the bridge's labored bouncing finally settled back to stillness, José opened his eyes and looked behind him.

The man stood at the edge of the bridge, his hands pushing out in front of him, clutching the railing, his feet planted firmly on the last inches of earth before that metal grate of the bridge began.

José took a few creeping steps farther along, tightening his stomach as the bridge dipped under his feet, but he kept going until he was halfway across.

He looked back again.

The man still stalled at the edge of the bridge, leaning forward as if the top half of his body wanted to go but his feet had vetoed the idea and superglued themselves in place.

If José had needed any more evidence that this man with the snake tattoo was indeed Vincent Goosen, he had it now. And he couldn't have been more thankful that Vincent Goosen was afraid of heights.

José took a deep breath. Then he took a step. And then another one. If he could get across, he could get away.

As long as Goosen stayed put.

Hand after hand, José reached for the railing, as if he were pulling himself along. One foot in front of the other, and again. He crossed the bridge's sagging middle until it finally sloped up to meet the trail — beautiful, solid, steady dirt — on the other side.

José looked back one more time. Goosen slid one foot onto the bridge and then pulled it back. He wasn't coming. He would never come. This bridge was freaky enough for a regular person; for someone with a fear of heights, it would feel like crossing the Grand Canyon on a tight rope.

José was safe. He took a deep breath.

Something rustled in the brush off to his right, and he remembered safe was a relative term. But he was as safe as someone could be in a rain forest full of deadly animals at night. And that was an improvement over a few minutes ago.

José took a few steps and surveyed three trails that split off into the darkness. He thought Sofia had led them off to the left before, when they'd gone to look for Alejandro at the cultural center.

The moon was watery and weak on the trail, and José didn't know if he could find his way. But he sure wasn't going back over that bridge.

There was nothing to do but keep walking.

SIXTEEN

Somehow, leaving Goosen on the far side of the shaky bridge gave José an infusion of courage as he walked the damp, dark trail. The rain had finally stopped, and it was weird, but he actually felt calm, maybe for the first time since he'd gotten on that plane back in Washington. No . . . before that even. Since his teacher had handed him that envelope with the paper that was probably all smudged and soggy in the bottom of his backpack by now.

Maybe it was the quiet of the jungle humming and buzzing, whispering to him like the white noise machine his mom turned on when he couldn't sleep at home.

José paused in a clearing and wondered what time it was. Two in the morning? Three? How long had he been walking? How long had he crouched under Goosen's window? How long had he stood frozen in the middle of the bridge?

It felt a little cooler. The clouds had thinned, and a half-moon lit the sky, but there was no sign of dawn yet.

The trail kept snaking to the left and the right, forking one way and another, and José tried to remember which way Sofia had led them, but he was getting tired. Thirsty, too. He longed for the water bottle he'd left way back under Goosen's window.

GRROOOO . . . a throaty voice croaked up in the trees. José searched the moonlit branches and made out a shape — some kind of bright white dragonfly or moth, wings glowing against the midnight sky. Could a bug be making that deep, growly sound?

He took a step closer, and the white wing shape lifted from the tree — but it wasn't an insect at all. José startled, then laughed. It was the big, white, feathery eyebrow of an enormous owl, pumping its wings away over the trail now.

José started walking again. He never would have seen the owl if it hadn't called out its deep hoot-croak. *There must be animals all around*, he thought. But instead of making him nervous, it made him feel . . . less alone. Like they were out there, hiding in plain sight, but on his side.

Finally, after he'd taken a lot more turns, and probably hiked in a few circles, José saw light shining through the trees ahead.

He started running — but stopped fast when he reached the driveway in front of the cultural center and found Alejandro waiting with a machete raised over his head.

"Who's there?" he growled, squinting into the shadows.

"It's . . . ah . . . it's me," José called weakly, stepping slowly into the light with his hands up. "José? Sofia's . . ." He couldn't exactly call her a friend. Not when he was all mad at her for whatever she wrote in her dumb journal and wouldn't show him. Not when he'd run off without telling anyone. "I was here with Sofia yesterday?"

Alejandro lowered the machete. "What in the blazes are you doing out at this hour?"

José stepped forward into the clearing. "I . . . came to see you. I was —"

"It didn't occur to you that prowling around this place in the dark the morning after a break-in might get you killed?"

"What? What break-in?"

Alejandro narrowed his eyes and looked hard at José, then seemed to make up his mind. "Somebody broke into the cultural center while I was at dinner with Juliana last night. I came back and found glass all over the place."

"Did they take anything?"

"Nothing too valuable, but they got three of my favorite masks and a couple woven blankets. Anyway, when I heard you crashing through the trees, I thought whoever it was might be back." He shook his head and leaned the machete against the curved wall of the building. "What are you doing here?"

"This guy was chasing me." José swallowed hard. "It . . . I'm pretty sure it was Vincent Goosen."

Alejandro stared at him for a few seconds. Then he plopped down on the bench outside the cultural center and pointed to the spot next to him. "Sit. And explain."

José sat. He told Alejandro how he'd been sort of mad at Sofia and Anna and Henry (he didn't say why), how he'd wandered to the office to go online and look for information, how the man at the desk had surprised him, checking in late, and how José had wondered — it was crazy, he knew — but he'd wondered if the man looked a little like the picture of Goosen he'd seen on the Internet.

"So you *followed* him?" Alejandro's face was full of admiration. "I underestimated you, little man."

José told him about the snake tattoo —

"Wait!" Alejandro jumped up, ran into the cultural

center, and came back out pawing through papers in a thick manila folder. "Did it look like this?" he asked, holding up a printout. It was the mug shot José had seen on television last winter when Goosen was a suspect in the Star-Spangled Banner heist.

"Yeah," José said, but he immediately doubted himself. "I mean, it was pretty dark. But there's more." José told him about being chased through the woods, about the bridge that Goosen wouldn't cross. "Because you know that he's —"

Alejandro was already nodding. "Afraid of heights." He whispered a curse under his breath. "He's really here." He held the folder in front of him as if Goosen himself might rise out of the papers.

"What *is* all that?" José asked. "You've got a file about him?"

Alejandro handed the folder to José. "I've been learning about him as long as I can remember. You want to defeat your enemy — you need to know exactly who he is."

José nodded slowly and flipped through pages that comprised a painstakingly detailed biography of Goosen, from the early days before he joined the Silver Jaguar Society, to his betrayal of the group in Montreal, and on to a long list of heists in which he was suspected.

There were paparazzi-style photos of Goosen walking down the streets of some city, drinking coffee in a café, hurrying along a subway platform. Even with his hair dyed black now, it was easy to see it was the same man with the same cold eyes.

There were pages and pages of excruciatingly detailed notes on Goosen's movements around the world.

"This must have taken forever," José said, handing the folder back to Alejandro.

"I have one for every member of his gang." He grimaced. "I . . . I wasn't sure it was *him* this time, but I had to find out. I figured I'd save a little money to travel, track down some leads. But traffic around here is so slow in the rainy season. I've been running extra tours. . . ." His shoulders sank, and he looked off into the trees. "And yeah . . . that includes some tours that Michael isn't thrilled about."

José's mind immediately took him back to the echoey tunnels of that cave with the rare spiders — the ones that Russian lady had paid to see. "So that wad of money you took from the Russian lady . . ."

Alejandro sighed and nodded. "That, and what the chubby bird-watcher guy paid me for his walk to see the macaw nest in the almendro tree — it was supposed to help me hunt down that Jaguar Cup."

"But what if you don't need to travel now? Don't you think there's a chance the cup is already here? With Goosen?"

"Maybe." Alejandro sat back down on the bench,

clasped his hands at his chin, and leaned forward, staring into the dirt for a long time. Finally, he looked up at José. "But if he *has* the Jaguar Cup, why is he still here?"

"Well . . . maybe he's hidden it."

"Why?"

"Well . . ." José didn't know. Wasn't that what bad guys did with things they stole? If Henry were here, he'd be able to quote Mad Ben the Pirate, or some video game where ninja nuns hide a stash of century-old diamonds in their habits. If Anna were here, she'd have a chart in her notebook that explained why. But they weren't here. "I guess I don't know."

"That's the thing," Alejandro said. He looked at his watch, paused, then seemed to make a decision. "There's only one way to find out if Goosen's got the Jaguar Cup." He reached for the machete leaning against the building and slid it into his belt. "You remember which room is his?"

SEVENTEEN

By the time they crossed the bridge, the sky had turned from moonlit blue to misty yellow dawn. Alejandro crept quickly but quietly, staying to the shadows along the path to the pool.

"Over here." Alejandro motioned José behind a tall plant whose flowers looked like something from another solar system. A riot of red-yellow spikes rose from sharp green blades that grew from the ground, all fanned out like a skirt for some exotic dancer.

They crouched waiting while the sun burned off the morning mist. A shining green hummingbird appeared, hovered near one of the blossoms, then darted away. José wondered what the flower smelled like. His legs felt cramped from squatting.

He looked across the pool toward Goosen's

room — still dark, still quiet — and carefully stretched out his legs, leaning in toward the plant, nose first.

"Stop." Alejandro hissed, and José dove to the ground, peering through the leaves toward Goosen's room.

But there was no movement. No sign of him.

José turned to Alejandro, annoyed that his heart was thudding all over the place. "*What?*"

"That hummingbird passed up that heliconia blossom for a reason, my friend," Alejandro whispered, and he pointed to the tip of the red-yellow bloom. "Look. From a distance."

José stood back a few steps to study the flower he'd been about to sniff. Coiled carefully atop one of the red blossoms was a skinny, bright yellow snake. It matched the plant's color so perfectly it looked just like another bit of blossom. José might have sniffed the top of its head if Alejandro hadn't stopped him. His stomach felt a little queasy as he squatted back down behind the greens. "Is it poisonous?" he asked, though he was pretty sure he already knew the answer.

"Venomous," Alejandro corrected. "That's an eyelash palm pit viper, and it's *venomous*. Poison is something that harms you when you eat it or touch it. Venom is something that harms you when it's injected with a stinger or spikes —"

"Or fangs." José watched as the snake wound its way down the blossom and disappeared into the leaves. "I didn't see it before."

"Neither did the hummingbird, at first," Alejandro said. "That snake blends in with the hummingbird's favorite food and uses that to hunt. It'll wait on the heliconia plant for a careless bird to come by, and then —" He struck out with his hand as if it were a snake attacking José's knee, and José jumped about a mile, just as Vincent Goosen's door swung open.

"Shhh." Alejandro put his arm on José's shoulder and pushed him lower to the ground. They watched Goosen lock his door and head up the walkway to breakfast.

"Should we go?" José whispered.

Alejandro nodded, but then held up a finger — *wait* — and pulled out his cell phone. "Juliana," he said, smiling into the phone. He said something else in Spanish, waited, said, *"Muchas gracias,"* and turned to José. "Let's go. I know someone — a waitress in the dining room — who's going to keep our friend busy talking for a while at breakfast."

José followed Alejandro past the door to Goosen's room and up to the window. His water bottle was gone. Did Goosen have it? The thought made his stomach twist. "What if Goosen doesn't want to talk to your friend?"

"Oh, he'll want to talk with Juliana." Alejandro grinned as he pulled the screen off the window and motioned for José to climb in first. "In addition to Goosen's fear of heights, he has a weakness for beauty."

José hoisted himself up — the window was right above his waist level — and let Alejandro give him a boost to swing one leg over the windowsill and onto the bed below it. He tried to keep his muddy shoes off the covers but with no luck. "Shoot!" he whispered out the window. "I got mud on the bedspread. He'll know we were here!" He slid off the bed onto the floor and tried brushing off the mud but only succeeded in smudging it.

Alejandro climbed in behind him, easily sidestepping the bed with his longer legs. "Don't worry. We'll flip it over and put this one on the other bed before we go." He stepped up to Goosen's suitcase and rummaged through, pulling out safari shirts, boxer shorts, cargo pants, and smelly socks. But no Jaguar Cup.

"What about the safe?" José asked.

"Maybe." Alejandro started toward it. "But he'd probably know that the lodge staff would have an override code for the combination." With a few quick turns of his fingers — apparently it wasn't only lodge staff but also friends of waitresses who knew the override code — he swung open the door to the safe. "Nothing but a fake passport and a stash of Swiss chocolate."

Alejandro knelt next to the bed and lifted the edge of the mattress. "I don't think we're going to find anything," he said, feeling around between the mattress and box spring. "If Goosen had the cup, I suspect he'd be long gone by now." Alejandro nodded toward the other bed. "Check that one, though."

Reluctantly, José slid his hand under the mattress, afraid he might find not the Jaguar Cup but some spider nest or sleeping scorpion nestled under there. Instead, his hand hit hard plastic. "Hey." He groped farther under the mattress. It was the edge of a box. No, a binder. He wiggled it out and put it on the bedspread. "He had this out the night he moved in," José said, just as Alejandro's phone vibrated in his shirt pocket.

"Yeah?" Alejandro said into the phone.

The binder wasn't fancy; it looked like José's math notebook, only newspaper clippings and computer printouts spilled out the edges, instead of quizzes with crummy grades. He flopped open the cover and found a yellowed newspaper article about the 1972 theft in Montreal. José turned the pages — one after another, news stories recounted the world's most notorious unsolved art heists. Was Goosen responsible for all of them?

Interspersed with the newspaper clippings were printed photos from museum websites. José recognized a few of the pieces as paintings that had been stolen from museums in Montreal and Boston, but the rest — was that the *Mona Lisa*?? He was pretty sure that hadn't been stolen — yet.

"Okay, okay," Alejandro hissed into the phone. "Tell me when he's getting up." He sounded nervous. But José couldn't tear his eyes away from the book. He turned another page — and froze.

There, in a newspaper photo that wasn't yellowed — not at all, because it was only a few months old — were Anna, Henry, José, and their friend Sinan and his dog, smiling at the camera after they'd helped authorities recover the Star-Spangled Banner after the heist at the Smithsonian. Why did Goosen have this article? He hadn't been involved in that theft at all, even though they'd suspected he might have been. Unless . . .

José flipped frantically through the pages. There — a photograph of his mother from a museum event in DC, and there — a newspaper clipping that showed Anna's mom and dad at some party. Even in the heat of the morning sun, José felt a chill that made his bones shiver. Goosen was tracking members of the Silver Jaguar Society, collecting information about them just like Alejandro was collecting information about him.

José turned back to the page with his own photo, and his throat went dry. Goosen hadn't been chasing some random kid who'd peeked in his window last night. Goosen knew exactly who he was.

"Alejandro?" José whispered. "Look."

He held up the binder as Alejandro's phone buzzed again. Alejandro jerked it from his pocket — "Yeah?" — cursed, and yanked the bedspread from the bed, motioning for José to do the same with the muddy quilt in front of him. "Quick — we have to switch these and get out of here. He's coming!"

José dropped the binder to the floor, gathered the dirty bedspread in his arms, and helped Alejandro flip it, muddy-side down, onto the other bed. As they were smoothing the clean quilt over Goosen's bed, heavy boot steps came clunking across the porch — fast.

José started for the open window, but Alejandro shook his head and pointed urgently under the bed. José understood — no time to get away — so he dropped to the floor and wiggled into the dusty underneath. He heard Alejendro scootching under the other bed. He heard the *snick* of Goosen's key in the door. And then he remembered the binder.

Reaching out as fast and far as he could, José snagged the edge of it with his finger and pulled it under the bed, hugging it to his chest as the door swung open.

"Well, if he's here, I haven't seen him," Goosen said. *He must be on a cell phone*, José thought. He listened, trying not to breathe, trying to ignore the dusty threads hanging down from the bottom of the box spring, tickling his nose. "You're telling me you have *nothing* for me? No photos? Nothing?"

Goosen's voice was deep and tight. José watched boots pace back and forth by the door, still muddy from last night's chase. Then the boots clunked right up to the bed — José could have reached out and touched them — and the box spring over José's head sagged right down to his nose under Goosen's weight.

"You're sure we got the right lodge?" Goosen's voice came from above him.

Slowly, without making a sound, José turned his head to Alejandro, who lay frozen like a corpse under the other bed, eyes huge.

"I need more than that," Goosen said, "and I need it today. Call Hugo and tell him this has gone on too long. I'll get you the phone number. This place is crawling with SJ operatives now, and if they find out —" He cursed and slammed his hand down on the mattress. José felt the whole bed vibrate above him. "I'll talk with you later."

José held his breath as Goosen's weight lifted from above him and the boots thumped across the room. The door slammed shut, and José looked over at Alejandro, who held up one finger, waiting, waiting . . . until the boot clunks faded away on the trail.

Then he scrambled out from under the bed and helped José up.

"You gotta put that back." He lifted the mattress and waited for José to replace the binder.

José paused, clutching it. Leaving those pictures here — pictures of his mom, pictures of him — felt too creepy, like Goosen could see into their lives. Like he had collected not only their photographs, but *them*.

"Come on, man. We've got another minute — tops." Alejandro pulled the binder from José's hands, shoved it under the mattress, and knelt so José could use his knee to climb out the window. "Go!"

José tumbled out onto the dirt and scrambled out of the way so Alejandro could jump down after him. They ran, crouched low, back to the poolside garden and huddled behind the tall heliconia plants to catch their breath. Within seconds, Goosen reappeared on the path from the dining room, then closed himself back in his room.

José turned to Alejandro. "He doesn't have the cup." He sighed.

"No, he doesn't have it." Alejandro agreed, squinting at the building as if he could see through its walls. "But he knows who does."

EIGHTEEN

"Here he comes again!" Alejandro whispered to José, crouching low and peering between leaves in the garden as Goosen left his room, locked the door behind him, and strode along the path that led to the dining room.

But instead of climbing the dining room stairs, Goosen turned off on the walkway to the reception area.

"Come on, but stay back," Alejandro whispered, unfolding his long legs and heading down the path.

José followed close behind, all the way to the footbridge outside the reception area, where Alejandro hopped down into the shallow stream and gestured for José to come, too. "If we walk upstream a bit, we'll be able to get closer to the desk without being seen."

Warm water seeped through José's sneakers as he crept along the stream bed to a spot near the reception desk; they could even hear a radio ad playing in the office.

José moved a branch to the side, just in time to see Goosen step up to the desk as Luci appeared from the office — she must have been working a double shift with Michael away. Goosen looked friendly at first, saying something that got drowned out by an ad for zip line tours on the radio, but his face darkened when Luci shook her head. He said something else, and Luci looked down at some papers on the counter, then shook her head again and shrugged. Goosen's jaw twitched, but his mouth smiled, and he said something else and turned away, heading back for the bridge.

"Don't move," Alejandro hissed.

They stood motionless, tucked into brush and branches, while Goosen hurried down the path, raising his phone to his ear.

"He's not here," Goosen said, and there was no mistaking the frustration in his voice.

"Who?" José mouthed the word at Alejandro, who raised his eyebrows and shrugged.

"Then your information is wrong." Goosen paused on the small bridge over the stream, leaning against the railing and facing away from José and Alejandro. "Unless he's got a new alias. Or he's freeloading on the property and never checked in." Goosen turned slowly, surveying the paths and the trees, as if he expected his mystery person to be perched up in the limbs of one of them like an iguana. "Did you talk to Hugo?" A pause. "Tell him to check again."

José felt something crawling on the back of his neck and started to reach for it, but Goosen turned so he was facing their side of the bridge, staring right past them into the dark of the trees. José froze and listened. "If he's here, I *will* find him today. And if he's not, I'd better have new information tonight. Got it?"

Goosen shoved the phone into his pocket so violently José thought it might come right out the bottom and fall into the stream. Then Goosen wheeled around and headed back into the reception area. This time, he didn't bother smiling — just barked something at Luci, and she handed him a copy of the lodge property map. He practically tore it from her hands and grumped back out, over the bridge, and off into the trees.

"Think he's going to look for . . . whoever he's looking for?" José asked Alejandro as they climbed back onto the bridge.

"I do," Alejandro said, "and so are we."

They followed Goosen at a distance as he hiked up to the lodge parking lot. They watched from behind a banana tree as Goosen peered into the windows of every vehicle, jiggled the lock on the night security guard's hut, and squinted through the glass.

They followed him to the dining room and watched from behind the hostess stand as Goosen sauntered up to the buffet table, grabbed one of the last banana muffins, and darted into the kitchen.

He emerged a few minutes later, taking a bite of his muffin and making a beeline for the pool.

Alejandro and José followed and crouched behind the heliconia plants while Goosen searched underneath the poolside bar. He scoured the tiny building where the clean towels were stored.

He searched the staff break room, the laundry building, each of the lodge's seven guest-room buildings, and three dumpsters. Goosen slipped climbing around the edge of the last one and disappeared for a few minutes but soon pulled himself out, cursing and brushing rice and beans off his backside.

He pulled out his phone, carefully wiped its screen, poked at it, and held it to his ear. "Nothing," he growled. "Nothing! I'm going to take a shower, and if we don't have new information — solid this time — I'm leaving in the morning." And he took off down the path to the pool.

Alejandro let out a long breath. "Whoever he's looking for is either long gone or hiding too well."

"Well, good then." José sighed and plopped down on a rotting log. He was sweaty. He was hungry. He missed his parents. He was worn out. And he was tired of everybody hiding everything. Goosen could run around for the rest of his life peeking in laundry rooms for all he cared. Stupid Anna and Sofia and Henry could keep their dumb secrets, too.

José kicked at a rotting mango that must have fallen off a tree and launched it onto the walkway, where it landed with a satisfying splat. He spotted another lump of old fruit with a dead leaf resting on top and stretched out his foot to give that one a good boot, too.

But before he kicked, the dead leaf took off with jerky, fluttering wings — blue wings.

José stared after it, lifting and dipping its way among the trees in flashes of iridescent blue until it was gone.

"Your first blue morpho?" Alejandro asked. He was grinning. "They blend right in when they're not flying, don't they?"

"Yeah." José stared at the spot between the trees where the butterfly had vanished. It was like the glass frog, camouflaged against its own eggs, the giant iguanas with skin like bark, draped invisibly over tree limbs. The owl in the moonlit forest. All hiding in plain sight.

What if . . .

"Morning!" Leo, the bird lady's husband, waved, shuffling down the path in one of those popular tourist safari shirts. "Any idea if they're still serving breakfast?"

Alejandro looked at his watch. "Supposed to end at ten, I think, but you might find a muffin or something."

Leo nodded and headed for the dining area.

José stared after him. "Alejandro . . ." It was probably another stupid idea, but at this point, it really didn't matter. "What if the guy, or the woman, or whoever Goosen's looking for *isn't* hiding?"

The blue morpho — or maybe a different one — fluttered through the clearing again, alighted on the log where José had been sitting, and disappeared into the brown.

"They're probably not hiding," Alejandro said. "They're probably gone."

"No." José shook his head. "I don't think they are." Somehow, he felt sure of it. "I . . . I know it sounds weird, but what if they're here, not hiding. But blending in." He waved his hand at the butterfly, and it lifted itself up on bright blue wings, jerking and flapping, impossible to miss.

Alejandro stared. And slowly, he nodded. "That would be brilliant," he said. "But I don't even know who we'd be looking for. We certainly can't ask Goosen. And he's the only Serpentine Prince who hasn't been seen in Europe this week. So . . ." He shook his head and shrugged. "You want to get something to eat for now?"

They didn't talk on the walk to the dining room, and they didn't rush. Stale muffins weren't really worth hurrying for. And José was thankful for the quiet. He wanted to remember that last phone conversation with his mom to see if there was anything else she'd mentioned about Goosen — anything at all — that might help.

"Wait." He stopped.

Alejandro looked over. "Yeah?"

"You said Goosen was the only gang member who could be here. What about former members?"

"Like . . . ?"

"My mom said there was only one member of the Serpentine Prince gang they couldn't track down this week, and it was Goosen. But then she said there was some other guy they hadn't been able to find. I mean, she didn't seem concerned about him, not compared to Goosen, because he's not a member anymore. But maybe . . ."

Alejandro frowned. "Your mom said this guy *used* to be a Serpentine Prince?" He stared into the trees as if they'd show him the man's face or name. And maybe they did. Because when he turned back to José, his eyes were on fire. "That's it," he whispered. "Mortimer Loupe."

"Come on!" And he took off running.

NINETEEN

With a bottle of warmish water in one hand and a stale banana muffin in the other, José jogged along the forest trail after Alejandro, all the way back to the cultural center. Alejandro paused to hold the door open, then darted inside, rushed past the little devil masks and carved gourds and costume displays, straight to the back-room office where he practically dove headfirst into a deep bottom drawer full of files.

"Here it is!" He pulled out a thin folder with a few torn-out notebook pages and a couple newspaper clippings. It was nothing like the thick file he had on Goosen, but Alejandro waved it triumphantly before he slapped the folder onto the desk and opened it right up to a front-page newspaper story. "Mortimer Loupe," he said, sliding the article toward José.

It was the London *Times*.

ROGUE ART THIEF ON THE RUN, the headline read. And below that, *Former Serpentine Prince Furnished Mansion with Stolen Treasures*. The newspaper was dated two years earlier.

José looked up. "So this guy *used* to work with Goosen but went off on his own? When?"

"About three years ago." Alejandro tapped the paper. "He fell so in love with the art he couldn't do his job anymore."

"He sounds just like Goosen . . . when he left the Silver Jaguar Society," José said.

"Yes and no," Alejandro said. "They have different personalities. Loupe is . . . well, he's not all there. He's obsessed with the art, the culture, and that's all he cares about. Goosen is more calculating. He's more violent, and if you cross him, he'll get revenge or die trying."

"So this guy — Loupe — used to work for Goosen? This says he used to steal art for the Serpentine Prince gang," José said, looking back down at the paper, "but started keeping it for himself." At the bottom of the article was a photograph of a lavishly furnished ballroom with paintings — was that one of the Monet water lily pieces? — covering nearly every wall. The side tables were ornately carved masterpieces, works of art themselves, and a large glass display case stood in the center of the room, but José couldn't make out what was inside. He went back to the beginning of the piece and started reading.

ROGUE ART THIEF ON THE RUN
Former Serpentine Prince Furnished
Mansion with Stolen Treasures

Investigators with the Police Nationale made a bizarre discovery when they raided a mansion outside of Paris this week — an opulent and illicit collection of historical, natural, and gastronomic treasures carefully displayed in what can only be described as a passionate tribute to the beauty of the French culture.

Police recovered not only such treasures as the Louvre's missing Regent Diamond but also a pair of horns from the now-extinct Pyrenean ibex, carefully chilled rounds of creamy brie from Meaux, east of Paris, an enormous black truffle worth tens of thousands of dollars, and a bottle of "Shipwrecked 1907 Heidsieck," the champagne noted not only for its taste but its story of disaster. The hundred-year-old bottles were on their way to the Russian Imperial family in 1916 but were lost at sea during a shipwreck and never recovered until divers found them in 1997.

"It was like a museum — the most lovingly, thoughtfully curated collection I've ever seen," said investigator Guillome Larue. "It's nearly impossible to put a value on some of these pieces."

Police have fanned out across the countryside now, searching for Mortimer Loupe, the man believed to be the owner of the property and now a suspect in countless heists.

Known in the shady art theft world as "the chameleon" for his ability to appear natural in any disguise, Loupe may prove to be elusive prey for investigators. A former member of the infamous Serpentine Prince gang, he reportedly broke ties with that group after making off with a collection of ancient Greek sculptures that he was supposed to have turned over to the organization for a black-market buyer. Since then, investigators have noticed a rash of thefts from art museums and other institutions featuring ancient Greek pieces. None have been recovered, though police say this raid has provided them with the best leads so far.

"We believe that through the sale of certain stolen objects, Loupe has purchased a number of extravagant properties throughout Europe, where he may be storing many of the other missing treasures," Larue said. "In fact, sources have told us that his collecting has become somewhat of an obsession. We would not be surprised to find all of the Greek treasures in one house."

José turned the newspaper clipping to see if it continued on the other side, but that was all. He flipped through the rest of the papers in the folder — a bunch of scribbled notes and a few grainy photos that looked as if they might have been taken with a crummy zoom lens. In one, Loupe had a thick mustache and wavy brown hair, and he wore a three-piece suit and looked like the teller at José's dad's bank. In another photo, he was clean-shaven and nearly bald, wearing paint-spattered overalls. And in the last one, he wore a big red nose and a clown suit.

"That was ingenious," Alejandro said, leaning over and shaking his head at clown-Loupe.

"What did he steal when he was wearing the clown suit?" José was imagining Loupe, strolling through the Louvre with his big, floppy feet.

"A lion."

"A lion? Like, a real one?"

Alejandro nodded. "From a circus tent in Belarus. Our best guess is that he's furnished one of his mansions as ancient Rome and wanted the lion for some sort of Colosseum room."

José squinted hard at the man in the clown and painter and banker outfits. He looked so different in all of them; no wonder Goosen couldn't find him. "He could be anybody, anywhere," José said.

"But Goosen thought he was at the lodge. Why?" Alejandro gathered the papers and closed the manila folder on the many faces of Mortimer Loupe. "Have you seen anybody acting weird?"

Yeah, José thought. *Sofia and Anna. Henry, too.* But he didn't think that was what Alejandro meant. "Well . . ." He tried to remember their first day in the dining room, letting his memory wander from table to table. "There's this Leo guy who's supposed to be here bird-watching with his wife, but he doesn't seem to care about birds at all," José said. "Maybe he's really —"

Alejandro laughed. "Let me guess . . . he hangs out in the bar looking for sports on TV?"

José nodded.

"Trust me. That's not out of the ordinary here."

"Okay . . ." Who else? There had been the Russian lady and her husband, but they were gone now, and besides, José had learned the hard way that they were only after photos of the cave spiders. "Everybody else seems like typical bird-watchers. Like that guy who wanted to see the macaws."

Alejandro nodded. "Yeah . . . he was obsessed with adding that bird to his life list."

José nodded. "He'll go home happy. He saw some other rare bird at the lodge, too — even Michael was surprised."

"Which one?"

"Umm . . . he called it a splendid something."

"Not a resplendent quetzal?"

"Yeah!" José snapped his fingers. "That's it."

"He said he saw it around *here*?" Alejandro frowned.

"Yeah." José paused. "Michael made that exact face you're making, like he didn't believe the guy or something."

Alejandro opened the folder and stared intently at the images of Loupe. He looked back up at José. "Is that guy still at the lodge?"

José shrugged. "I'm not sure. Probably. How come?"

"Because the resplendent quetzal is a cloud-forest bird. It doesn't live here."

"So . . . either that guy made a mistake —"

Alejandro shook his head. "Any real bird-watcher knows the difference between a quetzal and a parakeet." He closed the folder and shoved it into a backpack along with two bottles of water and a small camera.

"But a fake bird-watcher wouldn't." José tried to

imagine the banker/painter/clown dressed as a tourist in the jungle. It was possible. "You think it's Loupe?"

Alejandro hoisted the bag over his shoulder and started for the door. "Let's find out."

TWENTY

"Hello, Luci." Alejandro somehow caught his breath and managed to sound calm by the time he slowed his run to a walk and sauntered into the reception area at the lodge. "I must ask a favor, my friend." José hung back, trying to catch his breath while Alejandro explained that he needed to find the stocky bird-watcher. He held up the camera — the man had left it in Alejandro's truck after a tour, he explained — and asked where he might find his room.

Every time José decided he trusted Alejandro, another smooth lie rolled off his tongue. But this one felt different. They had to find out if that was Loupe.

Luci checked her list. The man was in one of the far bungalows, tucked away in the trees across the street. "But maybe you should leave the camera here for him," she said. "When he checked in, he requested the most remote bungalow and declined maid service. Probably best not to disturb him. I am sure he will come by, though, because he's called for a taxicab this afternoon."

"Is he checking out?" Alejandro's voice had an edge.

Luci shook her head. "No, he said he was to meet someone. He asked for directions to Tavern Banana Azul."

Alejandro frowned, and José could almost see the thoughts zipping around behind his eyes. But he smiled at Luci. "I'll see if I can catch him now. I'm sure he'll be happy to have it back."

"Who would he be meeting?" José whispered as they headed across the road to the earthen steps leading to the bungalows. "Goosen?"

"No." Alejandro took the steps two at a time. "Goosen's the last person Loupe would want to see. But he may have hired someone else to . . . acquire artifacts for him. If this is really Loupe we're dealing with, then the Jaguar Cup is probably only the beginning."

José pictured the cup in the center of a room like the one from the newspaper clipping. "You think he's stealing more stuff? Like to decorate a whole house?"

Alejandro didn't answer. He put a finger to his lips as they followed the path through the trees to a bungalow tucked in shadows at the end of the dirt trail.

Leaves rustled overhead, and José paused to look up. Half a dozen monkeys with white faces were chasing the one in front, who had a juicy piece of fruit sticking out of its mouth. The one with the fruit reached the end of a branch, and José figured it was about to get pounced on, but it leaped out into the empty air and caught a branch on the next tree over.

Fingers closed tightly around José's arm and nearly jerked him off his feet.

"Hey!"

"Shhh!"

Alejandro yanked him into a clump of bushes, clamped a sweaty hand over his mouth, and pointed to the bungalow, where the bird-watcher — was it Loupe? — stood on the porch, facing his door to lock it.

José pulled Alejandro's hand from his mouth and tried to catch his breath. He could feel his heart beating in his jaw as the man sauntered down the path.

When he was gone, Alejandro stood. "Let's go."

The bungalows were air-conditioned, so they had real windows. One of the windows was partway open, though, with an air conditioner wedged in its small rectangle. Alejandro tugged at it, then grunted as the weight of the appliance shifted into his hands and he eased it to the ground. José followed him, climbing in and swinging his feet to the side so they wouldn't have muddy bedspreads to deal with later.

But this room was already a mess.

"Holy . . . what is that smell?" Alejandro's whole face scrunched toward his nose as if to protect it, and José didn't blame him. It was the wet-too-long, moldy smell he'd noticed coming from his own sneakers lately, multiplied times about a thousand and mixed with a stomach-churning combination of rotten fruit and overheated zoo animals.

Local newspapers were strewn everywhere, some crumpled and tattered on the floor, some carefully folded and covering every surface in the room.

Alejandro picked up a helmet that hung by a strap from the desk chair. RAGING RIVER ZIP LINE TOURS was written on the side in permanent marker. "Looks like someone went zip lining this week . . . and decided to keep a piece of his equipment as a souvenir."

José walked up to a desk heaped with books, newspapers, and magazine clippings. "Here's an article about the Jaguar Cup." It had a picture of what might have been the real one or the fake — José couldn't tell. "He's got some ad for a native costumes exhibit. And one of those tourist guidebooks." Alejandro stood breathing over his shoulder as José flipped through pages full of color illustrations.

"Somebody circled a bunch of stuff," José whispered. A woman's traditional costume. A heliconia blossom. A brightly painted oxcart. It reminded José of the way he used to circle toys he liked in Christmas catalogs when he was little.

José turned the page and his breath caught in his chest. There was a display of masks like the ones Alejandro had carved — the masks that had been stolen from the cultural center. That picture, too, had been marked. José looked up at Alejandro. "Do you think this is some kind of wish list?"

"Maybe." Alejandro frowned, took the book and flipped to the next section — COSTA RICA'S NATURAL TREASURES. There, peering out from its hollow nesting hole was a bright and bold great green macaw, circled in thick black marker.

Alejandro cursed in a voice that was half whisper, half sob. Then he bolted for the door.

TWENTY-ONE

"Wait!" José caught up with Alejandro on the trail, grabbed his arm, and jerked him to a stop.

Alejandro whirled around. His voice was as sharp as his eyes. "What?"

"What do you mean, *what*? What are you *doing*? It's him, isn't it? It's Loupe. We can't walk away now that we found him! What if the Jaguar Cup is back there?"

"It's . . . I . . . I *can't* explain right now. I have to go!"

"No!" José backed away from him. He wasn't giving up. Not when they were so close. "I'm not leaving. I'm going back to his room." He started to turn but Alejandro's choked voice stopped him.

"You can't. Not alone."

"Come with me then!"

"I have to go." Alejandro squeezed his eyes shut, clenched his hands into fists, and stood still as if time had stopped for a second. "This is my fault." His voice was quieter, but his eyes were full of anguish. "I took him to the almendro tree."

And suddenly, the puzzle in José's head unmuddled itself. The themed mansion from the newspaper article. The guidebook turned wish list. Loupe had stolen those masks from the cultural center for his collection, and he was going to steal the great green macaw chicks, too. If he hadn't already.

"I have to go," Alejandro said again. "I *have* to get there first." He started to turn away.

"So we're supposed to let him *have* the Jaguar Cup?" José blurted.

Alejandro stopped and swayed, as if two people were tugging on his arms, pulling him in both directions. "Get Sofia and the others. Have one person stand watch — no, two — and grab whatever you find for evidence. Check the drawers. Check his suitcase, the beds, the safe —" He snapped his fingers. "Remember 47-62-12."

"47-62-12," José repeated.

"That's the override code. Works on any safe at the lodge."

47-62-12. José's heart thudded in his chest. "Do you think it'll be there?"

"I . . . probably not, but if you find it . . . if you find anything, get someplace safe, and stay there. I'll find you. Let's go!"

José followed Alejandro down the earthen steps, across the road, and into the reception area. Loupe was nowhere in sight.

"Hey, where's the fire?" Luci called, but they didn't stop until they'd crossed the bridge and reached the spot where the path branched off.

Alejandro pointed toward the lodge rooms. "Go get the others. Hurry. And be careful," he said, and then darted down the other path toward the bridge that led over the river to the forest.

José didn't wait to catch his breath. He ran, whispering a number with every step. 47-62-12. His sneakers clumped along the wooden walkways until he got to Sofia's door and raised his hand to knock.

But he paused.

He could hear the girls' voices, then Henry saying something, and then laughing.

José's chest tightened. Did they even care where he'd been all night and all morning? Were they in there making plans without stupid José to mess everything up with his dumb ideas?

The door flew open, and Anna appeared, hands on her hips. "Well, were you going to knock or what?"

"We saw you out the window and then you just, like, stopped," Henry said, jumping up from the desk chair.

"Where have you been?" Anna demanded.

"Henry said you were gone when he got up," Sofia said, swinging her feet off the edge of the bed.

"Uh, yeah," José said, as his eyes fell on the journal next to Sofia. She reached out and pulled it closer to her. José's chest tightened. "I got up early to take a walk."

"Well, it's good that you're back. We've been putting together ideas all morning, and we're totally on to something, I think." Anna gestured toward the bench at the foot of the bed. "Sit down and we'll tell you what we've got planned."

José looked at the bench. "No thanks." He didn't care what Alejandro said. He didn't want their help. "I'm going to get some lunch."

Sofia stood up and picked up her journal. "We'll come with you, and we can talk on the way. I think there's —"

"I want some time to myself," José said, backing out the door. "I'll see you guys later."

Later, like never, José thought. He'd do this on his own, But he had to hurry. Breaking into a run, he rushed through the reception area, across the road, and up the steps toward the bungalows. The path through the trees was deserted. Even the monkeys from earlier were gone.

Loupe couldn't be back yet, but to make sure, José pulled himself behind a tree close to the bungalow and waited, counting to ten, watching the door. There was no sound from the building. No light in the window.

José looked back along the trail he'd been following.

Deserted.

He heard something — a rustle in the brush behind him — and held his breath.

Go on, he told himself. It was only some rustling bird or a monkey or whatever. But he waited another ten breaths to be safe.

The trees stayed quiet. As quiet as the rain forest gets, anyway. Insects buzzed, and toucans squabbled overhead. But the path was empty. And so was the bungalow ahead of him.

47-62-12, José thought, and hurried to the bungalow door. It wasn't even closed all the way — it hadn't latched when he and Alejandro ran off earlier.

José pushed the door open, stepped into the room, and went straight for the safe.

47-62-12.

His hand trembled as he pressed the buttons on the keypad. Each one made a short, high beeping sound.

47. Beep!

62. Beep!

José held his breath.

12. Beep! And then there was a quiet electronic hum as the safe's lock mechanism released, and the door swung open, faster than José had expected, and something hairy came flying out into his hands.

"Whaaa!" He jumped, half juggling the tangle of hair until he realized it was one of Alejandro's masks. One of the little devils, guarding the safe. Guarding *what*?

José put the mask down on the bed and reached in to pull out two more. A colorful native blanket or tapestry or something was stuffed in there, too. José reached in and started to pull it out. His heart sank when he saw the smooth, metal back of the safe behind it.

But then the thick roll of rough fabric fell into his hands — and almost pulled him off balance. It was heavy. Way too heavy to be only woven fibers and dye. He lugged it to the bed and pulled at the layers of cloth, his heart pounding, his brain trying to reason with it. No, it's probably not the cup. It's probably not —

But there it was.

The size of both José's fists held together, with the face of a jaguar on one side and the smooth coils of a serpent on the other.

José cradled the cup with shaking hands and lifted it to the light coming through the window. Its shine was dulled by centuries of cave air, but still, it glowed as if a light came from deep inside.

The cup was empty, but somehow, it felt full. As if all the Silver Jaguar Society members who'd ever held it had left behind traces of themselves, poured their courage into the cup, even as they drank from it.

José's heart swelled. He'd done it. He'd found the missing cup.

He was holding it, just as they'd imagined back in DC, before they knew they'd been looking at a fake.

He felt its weight, imagined all the other hands that had held it through the ages. He didn't know the words that went with the real initiation ceremony, but he whispered his own.

"I, José McGilligan, promise to uphold the honor of the Silver Jaguar Society with wisdom and courage, and to do everything in my power to protect the gifts of my ancestors and all the artifacts of the world."

The cup seemed to pulse with energy, and José saw his reflection in the polished gold. He imagined handing the cup to his mother. How proud she'd be. And his dad, too. They'd probably —

José froze. Was that a footstep on the porch?

There was another one. And then a cough.

How could Loupe be back already?

José felt dizzy. With shaking hands, he wrapped the blanket around the Jaguar Cup, clutched it to his chest and looked around frantically.

There was no way he could climb out a window; the bungalow only had two, and both were in full sight of the porch.

He dropped to his knees, but before he could scramble under the bed, the door flew open.

TWENTY-TWO

"José, what are you *doing*?" Anna's face was so red her freckles had melted together in a big blotch over her nose. Her shirt was all sweaty under the straps of her backpack. Henry was doubled over, panting.

Only Sofia, with that dumb journal tucked under her arm, looked as if she could run another few miles. She squinted at José, then surveyed the bungalow. "Whose room *is* this?"

Anna's sharp eyes took in the guidebooks, the newspaper clippings strewn over the floor. "Oh my gosh," she whispered. "Goosen? I was right, wasn't I? He *is* here!"

"Nah," José said, struggling to his feet, still hugging the itchy blanket. He didn't want to let go of the cup. "It's this other guy Alejandro and I were checking out."

"Who?" Anna pulled out her notebook, and José made a decision. She could write her own dumb secrets in there, but he was keeping this one to himself.

"Nobody really. We thought he might have been involved, but . . ." José shrugged. "Couldn't find anything."

Henry knelt on the bed and reached across for the masks José had pulled out of the safe. "Aren't those Alejandro's?"

Sofia stepped toward José and pointed to the blanket all balled up in his arms. "What's in there?"

"It's nothing, okay?" José ducked around her toward the door. He wanted to leave, to go find Alejandro and —

"Dude, what's your problem?" Henry stood in front of the door, blocking his way.

"Seriously." Anna stood next to Henry with her arms folded over her notebook. "You're acting all weird."

"We're all on the same side here, you know," Sofia said quietly.

And that set José off.

"Are we? Because it sure didn't seem like you cared about having me around before. You two —" He jutted his chin toward Anna and Sofia. "And your secret notebooks. Oohh . . . don't show José. He'll get some dumb idea and lead us all into a cave full of bat poop."

Sofia shot a worried look at Anna.

"José," Anna said, "that's not —"

"Then what? You think I don't see you whispering and laughing?" He shot a look at Sofia. "You think I didn't notice that all of a sudden your precious nature drawings are top secret? You don't want to tell me what's going on? Fine. But don't pretend we're all working together because we're not."

He reached for the doorknob, hugging the blanket bundle with the other, but Henry's hand shot out. Those hours of video games had left him with seriously quick reflexes.

"Hey!" José jerked his arm back, but the blanket came flipping open, and the cup — the Jaguar Cup — slipped out. Right onto José's foot.

"Ahhh!!"

"Whoa!" Henry dropped to his knees and picked it up, gaping while José sank into the chair by the door and hugged his foot. His toes felt broken.

"That's it, isn't it?" Sofia sank to the floor next to Henry, dropped her journal at her side, and reached out to run her hand over the cup's weathered surface.

Anna stood over them, staring down, whispering over and over. "Oh my gosh. Oh. My. Gosh."

José's foot throbbed with pain, but more than that, his throat burned with anger. Why couldn't they have left him alone, with their stupid secrets and —

José's eyes fell on the love-worn journal by Sofia's knee. She was leaning in toward Henry, staring at the cup.

José lunged from his chair, ignoring the stabbing pain in his foot, and grabbed the journal. In the process, he knocked Sofia forward into Henry, who tumbled into Anna, who tripped forward and fell over the whole pile of them.

Except José. He limped to the far side of the room, already flipping roughly through pages of carefully sketched spider webs, drawings of feathered birds and snake curves.

"José, please don't." Sofia sat on the wood floor, rubbing her elbow, looking up at José and wincing as if he were about to hit her.

But José kept turning pages. There! There was the sketch of that iguana they'd seen on the first day. That meant whatever she wrote and showed Anna in the dining room should be —

Oh.

Oh.

José's shoulders sank, and the sharp taste of his anger soured into shame in the pit of his stomach as he stared at the page Sofia didn't want him to see.

He didn't want to look up at her, but he had to.

"I . . . uh . . . sorry."

Sofia had her knees tucked up tight to her chest, her forehead resting on them.

"Sofia . . . I . . ."

She wouldn't look at him.

But Anna did. She glared at José as she scooted over to Sofia and put an arm around her shoulders.

"Dude." Henry was shaking his head. "You are a serious jerk."

"I'm *sorry*," José said again. "I thought you guys were . . . talking about me. Because I'm dumb."

"José, you are not," Anna said. "That's ridiculous."

"I . . . uh . . ." He closed Sofia's journal and looked down at the monkey she'd sketched on the cover, dangling by one hand from the *J* in *Journal*. It must seem ridiculous, José realized, because they didn't know about the secret he'd been carrying all over in the bottom of his backpack. He took a deep breath, and the words spilled out. "Look, I did really crummy on my state math test this spring, so I have to do this extra help class for slow kids next year. I haven't even told my parents yet."

Anna scrunched her nose at him. "What does that have to do with anything?"

"It just . . . it made me feel really stupid."

Henry shrugged. "Dude, that's really no big deal. My friend Brad's in one of those classes, and —"

"It *is* a big deal," José blurted. "Because being smart is . . . it's my *thing*." He flung an arm out toward Anna. "You're the reporter." And Henry. "You're the world champion of that ninja game." And Sofia. "And you're the . . . the machete-girl who's not afraid of anything. I'm not any of that stuff. I'm not a jock. I don't play an instrument. I'm the smart kid. Only now I'm not. I'm just . . ." He didn't finish. He couldn't. He wasn't anything.

Sofia lifted her head. Her cheeks were tear-streaked. "You're one of the smartest people I ever met. And I thought you were one of the nicest, too."

"I guess I'm not that anymore either." José walked slowly to Sofia and handed back her journal.

"Dude . . . you're still smart. Seriously, you're the guy who found this." Henry hoisted the Jaguar Cup into the air. "Now what do we do with it?"

"You put it down. And don't make another move." The voice came from the open doorway, deep and sharp, as Vincent Goosen stepped into the room.

TWENTY-THREE

José's eyes darted toward the window, but there was no way they'd all be able to escape. This wasn't Mortimer Loupe they were dealing with. Alejandro's folder on Goosen was thick with violence; he was brutal with his enemies.

"Don't even think about it." Goosen's eyes were fixed on José. He paused, then lowered his gaze to Henry, still holding the Jaguar Cup. "I want you to put that cup down — right where you are — and then slowly stand up and get in the bathroom." He gestured toward the door at the back of the room.

"Henry," Anna whispered. "Just do it. This isn't a video game. He's dangerous." Her voice shook.

Henry pursed his lips and nodded.

He set the Jaguar Cup gently on the floor and pushed himself slowly to his feet.

"You, too! All of you!" Goosen pointed at them as if he held a gun.

Only he didn't. Did he?

José tipped his head to one side and stared hard at Goosen's pockets while Anna and Sofia scrambled to their feet. There was nothing particularly bulgy there. Did he have any kind of a weapon at all?

"In the bathroom. Now!" Goosen lunged toward them, and Henry led the way, with Anna, Sofia, and José scrambling after him to pile into the tiny bathroom in the back of the room.

"Look! It locks from the inside." Anna pulled the door shut and clicked the button. "At least he can't get to us for now," she whispered, and turned on the faucet.

"Dude, we're locked in a bathroom with a crazy art thief out there, and you decide it's a good time to freshen up?"

Anna rolled her eyes. "So he can't hear us talking. We need to figure out a plan." José could hear Goosen rummaging around in the other room. Would he break down the door and come in after them?

"It reeks in here!" Henry pulled his shirt up over his face.

He was right; it smelled absolutely putrid. About ten times worse than the bathroom at José's house after his dad had been in there with the newspaper, and that was saying something.

"Maybe there's a window we can open." José didn't see one, but at home, they had a window over the bathtub. He pushed past Anna and tugged back the shower curtain.

A tiny monkey leaped out.

"Gah!" José stumbled backward, and the monkey came with him, clinging to his shoulder as if José were a lifeboat in a stormy ocean. They landed on the floor by the door with a thud.

The monkey picked its head up, looked José in the eye, and peed on his shirt. Then it jumped from José to the toilet and back to the shower, where it dangled by one arm from the curtain rod, its other hand scratching its belly.

"I guess we know why it smells," Henry said, leaning forward to look at the mess of monkey droppings smeared around the shower. "No window. And clearly, this thing isn't toilet trained."

"Of course it's not." Sofia looked as if she might cry. "Someone must have taken it from its mother."

"Loupe," José said, still slumped against the door.

"Who?" Anna squatted down next to him. They could still hear Goosen on the other side of the door.

"He sounds like he's throwing things around out there. He's got the cup," José said miserably. "Why doesn't he leave?"

"Who's Loupe?" Anna asked again.

As quickly as he could, José told them the story,

from his mom mentioning someone who used to be part of the Serpentine Prince gang to the thick marker circles around the great green macaws in Loupe's guidebook. "Alejandro's pretty sure Loupe's going after the babies. That's why he took off, to try and get there first."

Sofia squeezed her eyes shut. "Oh, please let them be okay."

There was a scratching at the door. "Shhh!" José held a hand up, listening, but it stopped.

He told Anna and Henry and Sofia how he'd come back here alone after Alejandro left, how he'd found the masks and, finally, the Jaguar Cup.

"And then we showed up," Anna finished the story. "And so did he." She nodded toward the door, and they heard what sounded like a chair tipping over.

"Dude, this is like something out of my Treasure Tomb game," Henry said. "These rogue archaeologists lure you down into the crypt and then —"

"Shhh!" Anna clamped a hand over Henry's mouth.

There it was again . . . a wiry scratching sound at the door.

"What is he doing? Tying the door shut?" José hissed.

Henry shook his head. "He didn't have rope or anything."

There was a sharp sigh on the other side of the door. More scratching. Then metal clattering on wood.

José tipped his head. "Sounds like he dropped a —" His stomach twisted. "A coat hanger."

"Quick," Sofia pointed to the doorknob. José was closest to it. "See if that still turns."

José reached for the knob. It turned, and the door clicked unlocked. He kept turning and pushed a little. It started to open.

"Stop that!"

The door slammed shut so hard José felt the vibrations in his chest. His hand flew out and hit the button to lock the door again.

On the other side, Goosen cursed under his breath, and the scratching started up again.

"He's going to trap us in here," Anna whispered.

José stared hard at the tarnished doorknob, and his shaken nerves pulled together into something harder — something more solid. He was angry. Angry at Loupe and Goosen for everything they'd done and everything they'd stolen and everyone they'd hurt. And José was angry at them for making him feel stupid and scared.

"He's not going to trap us." José turned to Anna and Sofia. "When we were out there with him before, did you see a weapon or anything?"

Anna shook her head. "I didn't notice. But José, even without a weapon —"

"There's only one of him," Sofia said quietly.

"And four of us." José stood up. "Together, we can do this. In union there is strength. Aesop said that."

Henry nodded. "Like those ninja leaf cutter ants. Power in numbers."

José looked at the doorknob, blinking fast. "Henry, have you ever gotten past the rogue archaeologists in that game?"

"Pfft." Henry scoffed. "You just run at them full blast. That's like level-two stuff. I'm on level thirty-one now, but I can't get past the mummies. They're really fast, and —"

"Henry! Focus . . ." José's voice was sharp. Kind of brave sounding. He kind of liked it. He stepped up to Henry, pointed to the door, and whispered, "There's our rogue archaeologist. Are you with me?"

Henry's eyes lit up, and he nodded toward the door.

José started back that way, but Anna stepped in front of him. "You guys," she hissed. "I don't think we should do this. What if —"

"No." Sofia took Anna by the arm and tugged her back toward the sink. "We should. We can do this. We have to." She nodded at José.

He stepped softly up to the door, put his hand on the knob, and started to turn — quietly, and so slowly his hand ached. The scratching sound stopped, and José froze.

When it started again, he made eye contact with Henry and mouthed the word, "Wait."

Henry crouched back by the shower as if it were the starting line of a race. Over his shoulder, the monkey perched on the curtain rod, scratching its bottom.

José tipped his ear to the door. He could hear not only the scritch of wire on wire and wire on wood, but also Goosen's rough breaths. José closed his eyes. Those breaths got louder every time Goosen got closer to the door.

José heard a sharp huff.

"NOW!" he mouthed to Henry and turned the knob all the way to the right as he pulled his body into the corner of the bathroom, out of the way.

Henry sprang toward the door as if he were going to head-butt it, but at the last second, he threw his shoulder around, twisted his body, and threw his leg sideways — *"Eeyah!"* — into a powerful kick that sent the door flying open and Vincent Goosen staggering back, slipping on loose newspapers, and tumbling over the desk chair. He cracked his head against the corner of the desk on his way to the floor, landed hard on his back, groaned, and squeezed his eyes shut, clutching his head.

Henry ran for the door, leaping over Goosen's splayed out legs.

"Go!" José yelled.

Anna hesitated, but Sofia grabbed her hand and pulled her from the bathroom. "Let's go!"

José was right behind them, but as he flew toward the door two things caught his eye at the same time.

Goosen, rolling over onto his side.

And a metallic glint under the bed.

José hesitated.

"Come on!" Anna was at the door, looking back with huge, scared eyes.

But he couldn't leave it.

José lunged toward the bed. Just as his hands closed around the smooth, cool curves of the Jaguar Cup, one of Goosen's huge, hairy hands clamped onto his ankle.

José tugged, but Goosen's grip tightened like a vise. He grunted and pulled himself closer on his belly.

José tried again to pull his leg free.

Goosen held on tighter and wiggled closer.

José's heart thumped in his chest, in his throat, his eyes — everywhere. It pounded in his fingers and pulsed against the gold of the Jaguar Cup.

The cup!

José jerked his head up toward the door, frantic, and saw Anna holding out her hands.

"Grrah!" He heaved with all his might, threw the cup with all his weight behind it, and staggered forward, dragging Goosen along with him as he tumbled to the floor.

The cup didn't make it to Anna — it was so heavy it barely left José's hands before it thudded to the floor. But Henry leaped on it, scooping it into his arms before Goosen even had time to look up.

"Go!" José screamed.

"Hey!" Goosen's gruff voice called toward the doorway. José felt the grip on his ankle loosen the tiniest bit. He kicked out behind him as he hard as he could, channeling every video game hero Henry had ever mentioned, and connected squarely with Vincent Goosen's face.

Goosen screamed.

José scrambled to his feet, staggered out the door, and ran.

TWENTY-FOUR

Anna, Henry, and José had stopped maybe twenty yards down the trail, but when José came leaping off the porch, waving his arms, hollering "Go!" they took off again.

"We . . . were going . . . to go back for you," Henry panted when José caught up to them near the road. They had to wait for traffic. José bent over, hands on his knees, to catch his breath, while a banana truck and a bunch of cars and Jeeps behind it sped past.

"It doesn't look like he's coming," Anna said, looking warily back up the trail.

But José had a bad feeling in the pit of his stomach. After he kicked Goosen and took off, he'd stolen a look back into the bungalow and seen Goosen's face — tight and twisted not only in pain but in rage.

"Let's not wait to find out," José breathed as the last Jeep rumbled by, and he started running again. He led them across the road, halfway up the hill on the trail that led back to the reception area, where they could —

"Hold on!" José stopped so fast Anna ran right into him and almost knocked him down. "Where are we taking this thing?" He nodded toward Henry, who had pulled up the bottom part of his T-shirt to make a sling for the Jaguar Cup, then turned to Sofia. "Is your dad even back yet?"

She shrugged. "I haven't seen him, but he said probably —"

Tires squealed on the road below them, and José whirled around to see Goosen, his mouth twisted and bellowing, barreling across the road in front of an old pickup truck.

"Come on!" José took off running — not to the reception area but the other way — toward the trail that led across the river to the primary growth forest. They needed Alejandro.

He stumbled up the rest of the hill, sliding in fresh mud from last night's rain at the steepest part near the top. He found a root sticking up near the base of a tree, used it to pull himself up, and looked back. Anna and Sofia were right behind him, but Henry had fallen back, trying to climb with one hand and hold onto the cup wrapped in his shirt with the other.

Goosen had reached the hill. He was on the part that wasn't steep and slippery, and he was coming fast.

"Here!" Sofia took two steps toward Henry and held out her hands. He passed her the cup. "Anna!" She passed it up the hill to Anna and then José, at the top. He wrapped his arms around it and held it tight to his chest. His heart thumped against the gold, still warm from Henry's body, as the others climbed.

Sofia and Anna made it to the top. Henry was almost there, but Goosen was close, reaching out toward Henry's muddy sneaker.

"Watch out!" José yelled.

Henry grasped the root and tugged himself up. Goosen lunged, but his long, thick fingers clutched at empty air, his feet flew out from under him, and he slid backward.

Before José could even take a breath, Goosen was climbing again, though. His eyes were dark, his face smeared with blood and mud.

"Let's go!" José pushed through the underbrush at the top of the hill and burst into the parking area. He ran across the gravel lot and veered off to the main lodge trail, toward — where? Where were they even *going*? No place was safe.

José's parents and Michael weren't back yet, and Alejandro was off in the forest trying to save baby macaws. Who was going to save *them*?

"Luci! Luci!" Sofia hollered as they burst into the reception area.

But the desk was empty. And in the split second they paused to listen for Luci's answer, they heard heavy boots crunching on the gravel driveway, coming closer.

"Come on!" José bolted down the path.

He heard Anna, Henry, and Sofia close behind him, their footsteps loud and hollow over the little footbridge outside the reception area. Where the trail split, José veered left.

He gulped in deep breaths of midday air, more hot water than oxygen. When he reached the next split in the trail, he couldn't run anymore. He bent over, clutching the heavy cup, gasping for breath. One path led to the pool area, the other to the dining hall.

"I'll take it for a while," Sofia said, tugging the cup from his hands. But she looked as worn out as José felt.

Anna looked around frantically. "What if we go into the trees and hide?"

But there was no time. Goosen came bursting from the trees, around a bend in the trail, heading straight for them.

Sofia took off toward the pool, with Anna, Henry, and José on her heels and Goosen — would he ever wear down? — maybe twenty yards behind them.

It took all of José's energy to pull enough air into his lungs to keep going, keep running. He focused on the dark blotch of sweat on the back of Henry's T-shirt and repeated with every step, "Go, go, go . . ."

Suddenly, Henry stopped so fast José almost fell on him — and then Henry was pushing him, turning him back. "Go back! Go!"

José started running, leading now — why? He jerked his head and looked over his shoulder long enough to understand.

The pool trail looped in a circle. Goosen had wheeled around and doubled back so that for a second, they'd been running right at him. Now they were running away again, only —

José stopped.

Because Goosen had stopped. Now he started running the other way. José whirled and screamed to Sofia, "Go!" And they ran until Goosen whipped around and came at them again from the other direction.

Back and forth. The glimmering pool water mocked José — he was so thirsty. Spots blurred his vision.

"Go back!" Henry called suddenly, and José turned to follow him and Anna and Sofia, whose whole body seemed to be drooping under the weight of the cup she carried. José knew she couldn't last much longer.

"He stopped!" Anna screamed.

And they stopped, too, sucking in gulps of air.

Opposite them, across the pool, Goosen leaned forward, hands on his knees, as if he were getting ready to leap across and swallow them. His body heaved with every breath. His face looked as possessed as one of those awful masks.

And José's heart felt as dark as the masks' empty eyes.

It was never going to end.

Goosen lurched and started toward them again.

José ran. His knees trembled. Pain shot through his side, and with every step, he felt Goosen's eyes burning into his back. They were the eyes of someone who was never giving up. As long as they had the Jaguar Cup, Goosen would be after them. He would follow them anywhere.

Except —

"This way!" José prayed he was in the right spot. He pushed aside the heliconia plants at the poolside garden and stumbled through the brush. He could hear Henry and Anna and Sofia crashing after him. If he was wrong — if he was wrong, Goosen would be on them within seconds, but — *yes!*

José exploded out of the trees onto the open trail. Behind him, Henry burst onto the path, then Anna, then Sofia, a look of terror on her face. And a half second later, Goosen flew out of the trees behind her. He stumbled and fell to his knees, and Sofia rushed forward, pushing the Jaguar Cup into José's hands. "Take it!" she gasped.

He cradled it back into the already-bruised hollow at the bottom of his ribs and took off again as Goosen struggled to his feet.

"Come on! We can do this!" José screamed over his shoulder, then turned and ran faster than he ever thought he could.

He knew he was on the right trail, but still, his breath came easier when he rounded a bend and saw the swaying green bridge up ahead. A few days ago, he never would have dreamed of running onto that bridge. Now, he knew it was the one thing that could save them. The only place Vincent Goosen wouldn't follow them — *couldn't* chase them. On the other side of that bridge, the Jaguar Cup would be safe. And so would they.

José was afraid to look back again, afraid it would slow him down, afraid of what he might see, how close Goosen might be. He ran, clinging to the Jaguar Cup with his left hand, and flung his right hand out to point toward the bridge. They'd know. They'd be ready to keep running, and when they reached the other side, Sofia could guide them to the almendro tree and Alejandro, and finally, the weight of this cup bruising José's side wouldn't be all on them.

José was almost to the bridge — he had to slow down a little to turn but couldn't afford to hesitate for long or Goosen would be on top of Sofia — when he caught a glimpse of the river raging far below. His stomach twisted —

No, he thought. *No! Don't think. Don't stop. Go. Keep your eyes on the other side, and go!*

José sucked in a breath. He raised his head and fixed his eyes on the far side of the narrow bridge, and —

"No!" He breathed it aloud.

But the word didn't change what he saw — and even from across the river, he recognized the stocky rectangle shape of a man stepping onto the bridge on the other side, then breaking into a shaky jog.

Loupe.

There was no time to stop — no time to think. José ran past the bridge, through trees and down a steep hill to a swampy path along the river. Above its roar, and even over the whooshing of his breaths, he could make out road noises up ahead — trucks rumbling. It was their best hope now — get to the road and flag someone down for help.

José glanced back. The others were still with him — but so was Goosen.

José scrambled up a weedy bank to the roadside, set the cup carefully next to him, and reached down to help Anna, Henry, and Sofia climb up. But Sofia was shorter than the rest of them and couldn't reach the rocky outcrop they'd used as a foothold. She scrambled up, her boots making deep ruts in the muddy bank, but kept slipping.

Goosen reached the bottom of the bank, grinning.

"Anna, take the cup and run!" José hollered over his shoulder. "Henry, hold my legs!"

Without waiting, José dropped all the way onto his belly and wiggled out to reach down over the edge of the bank. He didn't look back but felt Henry's strong arms wrap around his legs to anchor him. He stretched both arms down to Sofia, caught her hands, and pulled as she kicked at the bank.

Goosen scrambled up a few steps and flung his arms toward her dangling legs, but Sofia's right foot found the outcropping and she pushed herself up. José scooted back on the bank and pulled again. Sofia's elbows dug into the soft mud at the top of the bank, but then her eyes flashed with terror and she twitched, kicking one foot down so hard it almost yanked her hands out of José's grasp.

There was a sharp grunt from below.

Sofia looked up at José and nodded sharply. "I'm okay."

He let go, and Sofia hoisted herself up onto the bank. "Where's she going?" She pointed to Anna, half running, half stumbling along the now-empty road. Whatever trucks had been passing by were gone.

José wanted to collapse on that empty road and squeeze his eyes closed. He had no idea where Anna was going or where any of them should go. There was no one to help and nowhere to hide, and he didn't have to look to know that Goosen was probably halfway up that bank by now. But José started running after Anna with Sofia and Henry by his side.

"At least this is better than trying to run over that bridge," Henry panted.

"No, it's not!" Suddenly, José wanted to punch Henry, but he kept running, his jaw clenched. He'd actually figured out a plan, and it would have worked, only stupid Loupe had to show up on the bridge because *nothing* ever worked for José. Nothing. "Goosen's afraid of heights — he wouldn't have followed us there. Now . . . now we're . . . we're finished." He felt himself slowing down.

"No we're not. Come on!" Sofia reached for his arm and tugged. She pointed to a roadside sign for a couple restaurants and tourist attractions. "The village is a mile or so up here, and there's a wildlife protection office."

José jerked his arm away and stopped cold. "We'll never make it that far. Look!" He flung an arm out toward Anna, who had slowed to a struggling walk ahead of them now. She looked as if she might melt into the roadside mud.

Henry had stopped, too, completely zoned out, staring at that sign for white-water rafting and zip lining and cheap tamales.

José squeezed his eyes shut. "We're never going to outrun him, and this is never going to end because he's never giving up. Never. That bridge was the only place he wouldn't have followed us."

José opened his eyes and gestured behind them. As if to prove his point, there was Goosen, pulling himself up to the roadside from the bank. He started running again, as if he'd never slow down.

"Dude," Henry tugged at José's sleeve, then pointed to the sign. "I think there's another place Goosen won't like." He turned to Sofia. "How far is it?"

She nodded and broke into a run. "It's close. Come on!"

TWENTY-FIVE

José had been sure he'd simply run out of steps, but he found a new explosion of energy and sprinted down the road to Anna, who looked wilted from lugging the cup along the simmering road.

But Henry took it from her, and she started running again, too, through a gap in the forest, along a mud-puddled gravel driveway, and across the open field where the speeding bikes of Adventure Racers had left deep scars in the mud.

The zip line tower stood in the middle of that field, looking ten times taller than it had before.

"Come on, it's totally safe," Sofia said, climbing the steep stairs. "I know how to hook everything up, and there's a braking system that'll slow you down on the other side. Just don't look down in the middle." Anna and Henry followed her.

At the top, Henry turned back. José was still on the third step. "Dude, come on. It's no worse than the bridge."

Totally safe. Totally safe, José repeated to himself as he clung to the rusty railing and climbed. Halfway, he paused. *Totally safe.* He pulled himself up another step, and his stomach clenched. He'd never understood his math teacher's explanation of exponential values, but now it made perfect sense how a seemingly small change could have a much bigger impact. Every step closer to flying off the edge of the platform felt a hundred times higher, a thousand times more dangerous than the one before it. It wasn't the climbing that bothered him so much as knowing what he'd have to do at the top. It was like those amusement park swings times a thousand.

Don't look back, José thought. *Don't look down.*

But then he heard pounding footsteps, and he had to.

Goosen was halfway across the field, sprinting. With tight white knuckles clutching the rails, José climbed — up, up, up — until he reached the others. Sofia was tightening a harness thing around Anna's middle, saying something about lines and clips and backups.

José looked over the edge of the platform. Goosen stood at the bottom, glaring up at them as if his eyes could shake them down like fruit off a mango tree. But he wasn't coming up.

"*¡Adiós, amigo!*"

José turned in time to see Sofia shove Anna off the platform, and his heart just about flew out of his mouth.

There was a high-pitched whirring sound. "Tuck your feet up!" Sofia shouted as Anna flew along the zip line, across the field to where it dropped off, then out over the river until she disappeared through a hole carved into the middle of the forest on the other side.

José thought he might pass out. He squeezed his eyes closed and felt the rough metal of the railing under his hands. There was no way he could do this. No way. He'd stay up here and they could send help for him later. Whenever. But he couldn't do that. He couldn't go flying out with nothing but a few straps of leather and —

"Uh-oh."

José opened his eyes and saw Sofia peering off the platform edge. "We better hurry. Henry?" She turned quickly, frowning, and reached for another harness and line. She handed Henry the harness and tugged at the straps until they fit snugly around his waist and legs, then grabbed a pulley-looking thing with handles and lifted it up to the cable.

José inched to the edge of the platform and peered down at the stairs.

Goosen was coming.

He was on the fourth step, clenching the railing so tightly the tendons on top of his hands bulged.

He looked up. His eyes burned into José's.

Then he lifted one boot.

Clunk.

And pulled himself to the fifth step.

José turned away and squeezed his eyes shut as the truth of being up here stuck in his throat.

There was only one way off this platform now. He couldn't stay and wait for help. Because who knew how long that might be? And if José could force himself up those steps, one by one, so could Goosen. José felt dizzy enough to tumble right over the railing. He had to sit down.

He lowered himself to the platform as he heard the *whirrrrr* of the zip line and opened his eyes to see Henry vanish into the black hole in the trees.

"You ready?"

Sofia was standing over him. He looked up miserably. "I can't do this."

"You have to." She pulled another harness from the shelf and held it out.

José forced himself to take it. Still sitting, he wiggled his legs into it, then stood up and held the railing while Sofia checked the straps. She clamped the pulley thing onto the cable and pointed to the strap that hung from José's belt. "That clips to the line as a backup. In case your main line fails."

She shouldn't have said that.

"José, come on." Sofia's voice was tight, and José understood why. Goosen was coming. And she still had to get herself off this platform, too.

José looked down at the stairs, saw only the top of Goosen's head, and felt the tiniest sliver of hope stir in his heart. Maybe Goosen wouldn't make it up. Each step, after all, was exponentially worse than the last. And five steps left a lot of exponents to go. Maybe José could stay put.

"You go first," he told Sofia.

"What? That's ridiculous. How are you going to set everything up? You don't know how to —"

"You can show me." José took a deep breath and stepped toward the cable, trying to look like someone confident who could actually handle this on his own. "Show me how to do it. Then go. I might not even need to use it," he said. "But if he comes all the way up, I'll go."

"And do what when you get to the other side? We can't sit there waiting for —"

"I . . . I can follow the river back to the bridge. You guys go. Find Alejandro. Get the cup to safety and get help."

"So you're going to stay here and refuse to move? Just because you're scared to —"

"I know it's stupid, okay? I know. But I . . ." José was close to tears. He hadn't eaten. He hadn't slept.

He felt like he was about to fall apart. "I know you don't understand. But I can't do this. Not unless I absolutely *have* to."

Sofia didn't say anything. But she nodded slowly, then raised her eyebrows. "And if you absolutely *have* to?"

José took a deep breath. He thought about the stairs that seemed so impossible, but that he practically ran up when he needed to, about the bridge he'd crossed more than once now, and he nodded. "If I have to . . ." He swallowed hard. "I'll be able to do it. Go."

Sofia bit her lip, thinking, then looked over the edge to the stairs. Goosen must not have been any closer because she nodded, quickly worked herself into her own harness, and showed José how to attach the pulley thing to the cable, how to lock the harness strap into it and how to attach the backup line, just in case. "You can hold on to the handles if you want, but there are two straps holding you, so even if you let go, you'd be fine."

"Good to know," José said, nodding. As if anything would be able to pry his hands off those bars. *If* he even went. Which he wasn't going to unless Goosen's hands were about to grab him by the throat. And Goosen seemed to be stuck on the sixth stair. *Stay there*, José thought. *Stay there.*

"Okay?" Sofia asked. "Did you hear me? Make sure that second line is attached." She pointed to the clip dangling from his belt.

"All set." José nodded.

Sofia kept looking at him.

"Will you go already?" He held up his backup line with the clip. "I'm all set."

"*Adiós, amigo*," she said quietly, then turned and without looking back, clipped her harness into the pulley-thing, and jumped from the platform.

The whining whirr of metal on metal as she flew away was the loneliest sound José had ever heard.

But it wasn't the worst sound. That sound came less than a minute later, after he'd lowered himself to the platform and closed his eyes.

Thunggg.

Thunggg.

Thunggg.

Step by echoing bootstep, Vincent Goosen was making his way up the stairs.

TWENTY-SIX

José's body felt electrified, as if every clanging footstep sent a bolt of lightning through the metal structure right into his bones.

He reached up to grab the railing, and his arms trembled, but he pulled himself to stand and forced himself to look down.

Goosen was halfway up.

Thunggg.

Halfway and one step.

José watched Goosen's chest rise as he took a deep breath. And another step.

Thunggg.

José took a deep breath of his own. He was going to have to do this.

Hands shaking, he reached for the pulley thing

Sofia had left him on the platform. He slid his feet one in front of the other, over to the cable.

Thunggg.

How many stairs were left? And weren't they supposed to be getting exponentially harder with every step? How come Goosen wasn't slowing down? Exponents were ridiculously unreliable, José decided, and felt a surge of anger at his math teacher. It helped him ignore how much his knees were trembling.

He lifted the pulley thing onto the cable and attached his harness. He gave it a tug. It felt strong. Stronger than he did. If he landed safely on the other side of this zip line, safe from Goosen and in one piece, he swore he'd hand the envelope in his backpack to his parents the second he saw them. He'd tell them everything and —

Thunggg.

Thunggg.

José tried to take a deep breath, but it caught halfway up his throat. He swallowed hard and looked out at the thick cable that stretched away from the platform. Then he remembered the backup line.

Thunggg.

Hands shaking, he reached down and clipped it onto the harness. He reached for the handles on the pulley thing and felt the smooth, cool metal under his palms.

Now all that was left was jumping. And flying. Soaring off this tall platform, over a ravine with a river full of probably crocodiles at the bottom, then into a black forest hole that was waiting to eat him. It still seemed like such a bad idea.

José waited for the moment he'd have to go.

But there were no more thung-steps.

Fine. He could stay here and Goosen could stay on his step two thirds of the way up the —

Thunggg.

A hairy hand appeared over the edge of the platform.

I could stop him, José thought, his breath coming quicker. *I could unclip myself and run over there to the edge and stomp on that hairy hand and he'd fall backward and maybe even get knocked out and then I could go down the stairs and get help and not have to jump off this platform and fly over the crocodile river and get eaten by trees.*

But José's hands were frozen, locked so tightly around the metal handle bars that they might as well have been superglued there.

Thunggg.

The hairy hand came up higher. It clutched the railing and pulled Vincent Goosen's whole filthy, sweating face above the platform edge.

He paused, breathing shuddery breaths, and stared right into José's eyes.

José tightened his grip on the zip line handles. His fingers were slimy with sweat.

"I don't even have the cup," he said. It was a last-ditch effort. He'd wanted to sound strong and mocking, so Goosen would realize how stupid it was to come all the way up here, so he'd decide to go back down, but the words came out high-pitched, shuddery and breaking, and made Vincent Goosen smile.

It was a snake's smile — all teeth and black eyes — and Goosen kept smiling as he pulled himself higher and finally — *Thunggg!* — stepped onto the platform, holding tight to the railing but breathing more steadily.

It was as if in that one pathetic sentence, José had handed this awful man — this thug — all the courage he'd had left.

No, José thought, gripping the bars tighter. He needed that courage — every drop of it — to do what he'd promised he'd do if the time came.

And the time was here.

Goosen cleared his throat, puckered his lips, and spit over the edge of the platform. "You're mine, kid," he growled, rubbing his hands together like some bad guy in a Saturday cartoon.

José felt a surge of emotion. But it wasn't fear. It was something hotter, more solid. *No*, he thought, *I'm not yours. No.*

Goosen took a step toward José, but hesitated. It was long enough for José to think of Eleanor Roosevelt for a split second. *You must do the thing you think you cannot do*, she'd said. Long enough for José to breathe in the super-charged air between them and take back the courage he thought he'd lost.

He sucked in a quick, deep breath — *"¡Adiós, amigo!"* — then threw himself forward, into the sky, into the forested air. He flew. Too fast to look down or pay attention to anything other than the wind roaring in his ears.

José's fear burst like fireworks, into something bigger and braver, and he let out a whoop as he approached the trees at the other side of the river and finally, let his feet down to meet the solid metal of the platform on the other side.

It was over in seconds.

There hadn't even been time to look back, and José felt a little wistful. He wished he could have seen the look on Vincent Goosen's face as he soared away.

TWENTY-SEVEN

"José, over here!" Anna waved from the trail. She was huddled with Henry and Sofia, not far from the platform. José was surprised to see them — weren't they supposed to be running the cup to safety and finding Alejandro?

The platform on this side was lower — no higher than a regular set of stairs — so José unclipped his harness and rushed down to them. Henry and Anna each had an arm around Sofia, supporting her as she limped along the trail.

"What happened?"

Sofia tried to put weight on her foot and grimaced. "I came in too fast and jammed my ankle on the platform."

"She twisted it pretty good," Henry said, nodding

toward the ground near a clump of trees. "Can you get that?"

The Jaguar Cup rested in a nest of leaves and moss. José bent down to pick it up but stopped short when he saw one of those big black ants — bullet ants, Sofia had called them before — scuttling over it. He used the strap of his harness to flip the cup over — a bunch more ants were swarming underneath — and carefully, flip by flip, hopping so the ants wouldn't get to his feet — rolled it away from the tree before he scooped it up.

"Well, that was graceful," Henry mocked. "You look like my undercover cop avatar when he has to investigate a murder at the ballet."

"You left it in a big ant nest, doofus." José started down the trail but realized that Henry, Anna, and Sofia were barely moving.

"You guys, this isn't going to work," Sofia said, breaking away from them and hopping over to another tree on her good foot. She checked for ants, then leaned back against its trunk, lowered herself down, and pulled her journal from her back pocket. "I'm going to draw you a map so you can go get Alejandro. It'll be too slow with me."

"You can't stay here by yourself," Anna argued. José wasn't sure if Anna was worried about Sofia or about herself, going on without her.

"But Sofia's right," Henry said, shrugging. "It'll take us forever to carry her out from here."

Anna folded her arms. "What if Goosen decides to come across?"

"He won't." José was sure of it. Climbing a platform and leaping from it were two very different things. And Goosen wouldn't be in a position where he had to jump to avoid being caught by some goon. "Besides, he wouldn't know how to hook up the harness or anything. There's no way."

"I'd feel better if we knew for sure he wasn't coming. Could we see the other side from up there?" Anna nodded toward the platform.

"Probably," Sofia said.

Henry took the stairs two at a time, then stood at the top, squinting into the distance for a long while, and finally raising his hand to shade his eyes. "There's somebody else up there."

"Besides Goosen?" Anna asked.

José dropped the cup by Sofia and darted up the stairs, already sure of what he'd see when he got to the top. He was right. A second, stockier figure was silhouetted against the sky next to Vincent Goosen atop the faraway platform.

"It's Loupe," José called. Loupe bent down for a moment, then stood, shifting his weight from side to side as he fiddled with something. The harness. "He's done this before. And he's not afraid of heights." José turned and ran down the stairs. "He's coming. We gotta get ready."

"You guys have to go!" Sofia urged, crawling forward with the Jaguar Cup cradled in her arm. She held it out to José. "Take it and go. I'll hide. I'll disappear in a hollow tree or something, but —"

"We're not leaving you here." José squeezed his eyes closed and held up his hand. He needed to think. His brain was flipping through all the newspaper articles from Alejandro's files, all the web pages he'd read about the Serpentine Princes, and Goosen, and Loupe — and in his mind, all the jagged details came together like puzzle pieces to show José the one big difference between the two rivals. "I have an idea." José's heart pounded; he knew it wouldn't be long before they heard the zing of the zip line. They didn't have more than a minute or two. "Alejandro says Goosen is violent by nature, angry and volatile and vengeful. But Loupe . . . From everything I've read, Loupe is crazy — he's obsessed — but he's never been violent except once when a museum guard surprised him during a heist. He's only dangerous when he doesn't get what he wants."

"So you're saying we *give* it to him?" Henry's mouth fell open.

"I'm saying that nothing he wants is more important than us." José gestured toward Sofia. "And if we give him the cup, then . . ." He hated the idea of losing, but there was nothing else they could do. "Maybe someday the Silver Jaguar Society can get it back. Right now, we have to look out for one another."

"He's right," Sofia said, pushing herself up to her good foot. José was surprised; he'd expected her to keep arguing for them to leave, but she hopped over to Anna. "Give me your backpack, okay?"

"Dude . . ." Henry's mouth hung open. "We're going to give it to him *and* make it easier for him to carry?"

"You guys, go back to the platform and check where he is." Sofia's machete-girl voice was back. She grabbed Anna's backpack and hopped over to the tree with the ants.

"Hey, watch out for those ants. They were —"

"I live here, remember? I know to watch for ants. Now go! See how much time we have!"

José rushed up the platform stairs after Henry and squinted into the sun. "Can you see what they're doing?"

"Not really. They're both still there, though."

"Yeah." José wished he had binoculars. "I think Loupe's the one on the right. With his arms up."

"Hey, it looks like he might be —"

Before Henry could finish his sentence, one of the figures jumped from the platform. Immediately, José felt the cable vibrating.

"He's coming *now*!" José yelled as he and Henry flew down the stairs. The dental-drill whine of metal on metal grew louder. How long had it taken José to fly across? Ten seconds? Twenty?

They ran to the girls. Sofia held the unwrapped Jaguar Cup, glowing and cradled in her arms. They all stared up at the platform, waiting as the whirring got louder. The backpack sat on the ground a few feet in front of them. José started to reach for it, but Sofia grabbed his sleeve and yanked him back. "Don't!"

"But I thought —"

"Look!" Henry pointed to the platform as Mortimer Loupe's feet touched down. His face was red and blotchy, but his eyes were bright. They almost glowed as he unhooked himself and bounded down the steps.

"Hold on!" Sofia raised the Jaguar Cup as if it were a talisman that could freeze Loupe in his tracks. And somehow, it did. He stood transfixed as Sofia hopped forward.

She sank to the ground, dropped the cup into the backpack and quickly — as if the bag were too hot to touch — zipped it shut and then backed away on her hands and knees, back to Anna and José and Henry. "There," she said, eyes brimming with tears. José couldn't tell what was hurting, her ankle from the zip line accident, or her heart from giving away the cup. "Take it, and leave us alone."

Loupe stepped up to the backpack, lifted it, and paused. His face lit up, as if simply the weight of the golden cup filled him with energy. "Thank you, my dear."

He flung Anna's backpack over one shoulder and took off running down the trail.

They watched him go until the thumping of his feet and the slapping of the backpack against his shirt faded to nothing but forest sounds. Frog chirps and birdcalls and humming insects. Jungle quiet.

José stood up first, brushed off his pants, and climbed the stairs once more. The platform on the other side of the river stood empty.

"Goosen's gone, too," he said, coming back down. "We might as well start hiking out."

"You're right," Sofia said, pushing herself up. Anna reached out to pull her to her feet, and Sofia grinned. She held out her other arm for José, who helped her start limping — slowly — down the trail that led to the village. He was surprised she wasn't more upset, but he figured he'd leave it alone for now.

Henry couldn't let it rest, though. "Dude, how are you *okay* with this?" He threw his hands in the air. "You're all machete-girl with snakes and then you just give up the goods to the bad guys?"

"She got hurt, Henry," Anna said, "and we're all tired. Leave it alone." She smirked at Sofia, and José shook his head. More girl secrets.

Henry made a noise that sounded like a cross between a laugh, a sob, a sigh, and a hiccup. "Well, what if Goosen circles around on the trail? What if he catches Loupe and ends up with the cup?"

"We did everything we could, Henry." Sofia shrugged and grinned at Anna. "I think it's safe to say that whoever ends up with that backpack will totally deserve it."

TWENTY-EIGHT

By the time Anna, Henry, José, and Sofia limped into a tiny village restaurant, they were soaked from the rain, hungry, thirsty, and exhausted. Their feet throbbed with blisters, and their arms crawled with mosquito bites. It was getting dark, and the local hotspot was buzzing not with insects but with news of a stocky European man who had come blustering out of the forest a couple hours earlier.

"He look like he have no neck. No neck at all!" exclaimed the lively older woman who was pushing plates of rice and beans and chicken at the kids from across the counter. "He come running up to the pilot at the airstrip — all sweaty and smelling." She waved her hand in front of her wrinkled nose. "He say he want to charter a plane — leave immediately for airport in San José."

Turns out this man with no neck wasn't in the plane two minutes — the pilot was still checking his instruments, getting ready to start the engine — when the guy started screaming in his seat.

"He wave his hand here and there as if he got a shark biting him and trying to shake off, you know? And he stare down in his backpack like it possessed! And he start to get up — but then he no move! Like the devil himself got hold of him!" Her eyes were huge. "You want more rice and beans?"

The kids all nodded. She served up another scoop and finished her story.

She told them the pilot couldn't take off under those circumstances. He certainly wasn't going to touch the man's backpack after what had happened to him — "Who knows what he have in there?" — so the pilot called the local police, who donned thick gloves before removing the backpack from the plane and emptying it onto the muddy runway. They did not pour out the devil himself. Only leaves and moss and mud . . . and the bullet ants that Sofia had scooped into the bag back in the forest.

And of course, they found the Jaguar Cup as well.

"Wow," Sofia said, reaching for her Coke. "Where's that guy now? The screaming guy from the plane?"

"Oh." The woman waved her hand in the air in front of her, as if this part of the story were hardly worth her time. "They throw him in jail. He be there a long time." She held up a serving spoon. "You want more chicken?"

They all nodded. Saving an ancient artifact, it turns out, really works up an appetite.

They were digging into caramel flan when Alejandro came running in with a lumpy burlap sack in his hand.

"Thank God!" he said, and wrapped his free arm around Sofia. He stepped back to look at them. "When I heard that Loupe had the cup, I thought . . ." He shook his head. "You're okay. That's what matters. What happened?"

José started the story where Alejandro had left him, in Loupe's bungalow. Anna and Sofia and Henry joined in.

"And he had a monkey in the bathroom," Sofia said. "A baby capuchin."

"So then I kicked the door open on Goosen." Henry jumped from his bar stool to reenact his heroic kick, grinning. "I'd always wanted to try that in real life. And it totally worked!"

They told Alejandro about the chase through the trails, about José's plan to ditch Goosen at the bridge, and how it failed when Loupe showed up.

"He must have seen me," Alejandro said, smacking his forehead with his hand. "Go on."

Anna told him about scrambling up the bank and running for the zip lines. José told him how he waited to jump at the very last second, when Goosen pulled himself up onto the platform, and how Sofia got hurt and then Loupe showed up. And finally, Sofia told him how she'd used a piece of bark to scoop the bullet ants into the backpack.

Alejandro's eyes were huge. "So then you sent Loupe on his way, and he got the sting of his life on that airplane while you four walked out of the woods and ended up here." He whistled, grinning and shaking his head. "And that's that."

But that wasn't all. "What about Goosen?" José asked. "Did somebody find *him*?"

Alejandro shook his head. "All the stuff in his room is still there, but he's — we don't know. He's gone."

The room was warm, but José felt a chill creep into his shoulders. Goosen was still out there with those eyes. He would probably never forget who stole the cup out from under him.

"But look who I did find," Alejandro said, interrupting José's worry. Carefully, he leaned in and loosened the top of the burlap bag. A fuzzy, feathery green head popped out.

"Oh!" Sofia's eyes filled again. This time, she wasn't acting; the tears were real. Happy ones, José could tell. "They're okay!"

Alejandro nodded. "Loupe slipped a teenager with climbing spikes three hundred bucks to go up and get them while the mother and father birds were away from the nest. I got there as the kid was climbing down with them."

"What a jerk," Henry muttered, reaching out to touch the bird.

Alejandro pulled the bag back from him. "If you saw how some of these kids live, what their houses look like, what they have to eat — and what they *don't* have — you'd hold off on the judgment."

Sofia put a hand on Henry's arm. "It doesn't make it right, but it — well, three hundred dollars is more than some people here earn in a year. That's why it's such a fight to keep the nests protected."

Alejandro nodded, then looked down, shifting his weight from foot to foot, and José remembered that he was the one who had taken Loupe to the nest to begin with.

Alejandro took a deep breath. "Anyway, Loupe was supposed to meet the kid at the bridge, but I bet he saw me and took off. That must be when he came running after you."

"Or after Goosen," José said. "It was hard to tell who was chasing who by then."

"I went straight back to the lodge to find you," Alejandro said, "but you — well, you know you weren't there. We've been searching the primary forest, just in case. Anyway, thank God you're all here and okay." He looked at his watch. "I've got an hour before it gets dark, and I need to get these birds back to their nest. Their parents have probably been freaking out. And speaking of worried parents . . . there's somebody back at the lodge waiting to see you guys, too."

TWENTY-NINE

José had survived his brushes with giant cockroaches, venomous snakes, spooky hooting shadows, and two of the world's most notorious criminals. He'd navigated the treacherous, winding paths of the rain forest at night, the stomach-twisting sway of the rickety bridge, and his death-defying leap from a towering platform to fly over a river.

But when he made it back to the lodge, the love-and-worry-fueled squeeze of his mother's hug nearly suffocated him.

José was gasping for breath, and the other parents were all hugging and crying and blabbering, too, so he only heard bits and pieces of what his mom was saying.

". . . can't believe he was here all that time . . . never should have brought you . . . don't know what Michael was thinking . . . Goosen . . . more dangerous than ever now . . ."

"Wait, what?" José managed to wiggle out of his mom's death-hug to look at her. "Why is Goosen going to be more dangerous?" José, who would never forget Goosen's angry eyes burning into him, already had that feeling. He wanted to know why his mom thought so, too.

She pressed her lips together, then nodded slightly as if she'd decided he needed to know. "Mortimer Loupe has promised to cooperate with the police in exchange for a lighter sentence. He's already told society members about a number of Serpentine Prince hideouts and storage facilities. If he's telling the truth, federal agents in Amsterdam, Paris, and Geneva will have raided three of those locations before Goosen even gets back to Europe."

"Well, that's great, right?" José was confused. "And if they know all that, won't they arrest Goosen at the airport or something?"

José's mom shook her head. "Vincent Goosen doesn't book an economy seat on US Airways when he travels, my dear." She looked at her watch. "He's probably long gone, on a puddle jumper out of one of the villages, or a helicopter that'll take him up into Nicaragua or Panama and back to Europe on a private jet or . . ." She shrugged. "Who knows . . . maybe even a boat from there. If he were easy to catch, we'd have had him a long time ago."

"So he'll be . . . out there." José thought about that.

"Out there. And furious." Then his mom gave her head a little shake as if she could make the thought — and Goosen — disappear. "But you know what? We're going to head home to Vermont in the morning, and —"

"And have something other than rice and beans for dinner tomorrow," José's dad said, joining them by the reception desk. He put an arm around José's shoulder. "I know Mom's chewed your ear off with how worried she was, but you should know that we're very proud of you, too. Alejandro called us to fill us in when he found you, and I am totally in awe of my brave, smart kid."

José leaned into his father's embrace and took a deep breath. "I have to tell you guys something. Not about what happened here. From . . . before we left."

His dad stepped back and looked at him. "Sure. What's up?"

His mom tipped her head, waiting.

"I . . ." It shouldn't matter now, but it did, and the truth got stuck in José's throat as if he'd swallowed that whole wadded-up paper from his backpack. But he didn't want to carry it around anymore, so he forced it out. "I got this paper from my math teacher, and . . . I kind of had a hard time this year, so . . ." He took another deep breath.

"Is this about your academic intervention class for next fall?" his mom asked. And she asked it matter-of-factly, as if she were asking some regular question like "How's that book you're reading?" or "Do you want a sandwich for lunch?"

"Yeah." José stared at her. "You knew about that?"

His mom nodded. "We got a copy in the mail two weeks ago. We were going to wait until we got home from the DC trip and then see if you wanted to get some tutoring over the summer."

"Oh." It was weird, José thought, suddenly finding out your heavy-as-lead secret wasn't even a secret. Like when you get to the top of a flight of stairs and think there are more steps up but really there aren't and so your foot sort of drops through the air. "Okay. Yeah . . . tutoring would probably be good."

His dad nodded. "We'll set it up when we get home." He shook his head. "Exponents, huh? Exponents kicked my butt in seventh grade, too. You know, it wasn't until high school that I figured things out and starting getting decent grades in math."

"Really?" José couldn't imagine his math-science-geek dad being anything other than brilliant in math and . . . well, everything. "Cool. I mean . . . I guess that means there's still hope for me, huh?"

His dad laughed. "You're light-years ahead of where I was at your age."

"Listen, we've booked a flight out of San José tomorrow," José's mom said. "We'll need to leave early, and we should get some rest. Dad and I are checked into a room near the river. Do you want to get your stuff and move in with us?"

José looked over at Henry, still trapped in an Aunt Lucinda bear hug. "I think I'll stay where I am for tonight. I won't see these guys for a long time, probably. Is that all right?"

"Sure thing." His mom gave him one more hug — this one felt a little less like being seized by a giant python — and ruffled his hair. "Expect a knock on your door bright and early. The van leaves for the airport at seven."

Back in the room, the night rain pounded the roof as José and Henry packed, tossing slimy sneakers and still-damp clothes into suitcases.

"Dude, everything I own is covered in mud. My dad's gonna flip when he goes to do the laundry." Henry sniffed at one of his socks and collapsed dramatically to the floor.

José laughed. "Hey, they could have come along. Then all their clothes could be growing mold by now, too." He sank down on the bed and reached for his book.

"Yeah," Henry said. "I hope Bethany's better. She's been throwing up a bunch. Dad's been all nervous and weird about it." He tossed a wet sock ball into his suitcase and started toward the room safe, then stopped and looked back at José. "You want the bathroom first or second?"

"Uh . . . second, I guess. I gotta find my toothbrush." He went to his suitcase and watched Henry walk into the bathroom. The door clicked shut.

José looked at the safe.

47-62-12. He still remembered.

But no.

José found his toothbrush, sat back down on the bed, and waited for the bathroom door to open.

"Hey, Henry . . . what's in the safe?"

"What?" Henry hurried to his suitcase, suddenly intent on rearranging his dirty socks.

"I said, what's in the safe? You've been all weird about it, and I . . . even if you got a crummy grade on a test or something, it's not that big a deal."

"Huh?" Henry tipped his head and looked at José like he was nuts.

José sighed and went to his backpack. "Look," he said, pulling out the crumpled paper. It was practically growing mold now, too, just like Henry's socks. "Remember I said I have to do that extra-help math class next year? I was afraid to tell my parents, but it turns out they already knew, and . . . Where is there dignity unless there is honesty?"

Henry tipped his head. "Quote from Shakespeare? Or is that another one from your mom?"

"It's supposedly from this ancient Roman guy, Cicero. But that doesn't matter. What I wanted to say is that if you have a secret, and you want to share it, you can trust me."

Henry looked at José for a minute. "You promise?"

José nodded.

"I got Randall in there," Henry said.

"Randall?"

"I figured you guys would laugh." Henry shuffled to the safe, pushed a few buttons, and after the lock clicked open, pulled out an extremely well-worn pink-and-purple stuffed animal.

It only had one sort of stretched-out ear, and José couldn't tell what it was supposed to be. "Is that a . . . teddy bear?"

"No." Henry sounded disgusted. "It's a bunny rabbit."

"Oh! I'm sorry. I see now." José tried to look serious. You couldn't very well promise somebody could trust you with his secrets and then burst out laughing when you found out the secret was a girly colored bunny rabbit.

"I've had him forever," Henry said, leaning Randall gently against his pillow. He looked at José. "You probably noticed he's all pink and stuff, huh?"

"Uh . . . not really." José shrugged.

Henry laughed a little. "When my mom was pregnant with me and she went for her first ultrasound thing, the doctor told her I was a girl. So she got all excited and went out and bought Randall. He wasn't named Randall then, obviously. He was just, you know, the bunny or whatever. But Dad says they found out a month later I was really a boy so they got me a whole bunch of boy stuff. And shoved this guy in a closet." He pulled Randall into his lap. "I found him when I was two, and I loved him even though he's all . . . girly and stuff. He's still cool." He gave Randall a squeeze and shrugged. "So yeah . . . we hang out."

"That's cool." José nodded, and then he yawned. He got into bed and only read a page of *Harry Potter and the Order of the Phoenix* before his eyes started to close.

"José?" Henry called.

"Yeah?"

"If you tell anybody about Randall, I'll have to ninja kick you across the room or something."

"Understood," José said. "Good night, Henry." He paused. "Good night, Randall."

THIRTY

José's collar made his neck all sweaty and itchy. "Can't I take off this tie?" he asked as they crossed the street to the Museum of Fine Arts in Boston.

His mom shook her head. "I know it's hot." It was insanely hot for September. Fall in New England was supposed to be crisp and cool, not all sweaty. It felt as if the summer rain forest weather had come to visit along with the pre-Columbian gold exhibit. "But you really need to look nice. You three are going to be the center of attention, after all. Look." She pointed to the huge banner that hung outside the museum.

CULTURE AND COLUMBUS:
TREASURES OF THE NEW WORLD GRAND OPENING
WITH SPECIAL GUESTS SEPTEMBER 4TH.

"How are they going to like it when their special guests pass out from heatstroke?" Henry grumbled, tugging at his own tie, but his aunt Lucinda hustled him up the wide steps toward the museum entrance.

Henry's dad laughed. "Hang in there; it'll be air-conditioned inside." He held Bethany's elbow as she climbed the steps, one hand on her belly.

It turned out Henry's dad and stepmom had been keeping a secret of their own while Henry had Randall hidden in the safe in Costa Rica. Bethany was never sick; she was pregnant.

"When's she having the baby?" Anna asked Henry.

"Beginning of December."

Anna smiled. "I always thought you'd be a pretty good big brother."

"Yeah, well . . ." Henry shrugged, but he looked pleased. "I hope it's a boy. I'm gonna teach him every SuperGamePrism cheat code I know."

"You ready for this?" Anna's mom pulled open the door.

José stood at the entryway, feeling half air-conditioned-cool, half outdoor-sticky, and stared at the red velvet rope that lined the museum entry for the special gala. "Do you think people will be disappointed about the Jaguar Cup?"

His mom nodded thoughtfully. "Some probably will. But anyone who knows the history, I think, will understand."

"You have to admit, the exhibit won't be the same without it," Anna said. "Couldn't they have set up really good security?"

Henry's aunt Lucinda shook her head. "That cup is too precious. The gold itself is one thing, but its historical and symbolic values are priceless."

"Don't forget Mortimer Loupe already managed to steal the Jaguar Cup while it was in transit once," Anna's mom said, "in the custody of a Silver Jaguar Society member, no less."

"But isn't Loupe in prison?" José asked.

"Sure," Henry's aunt said, "but he's one of many who would love to get their hands on it. If one of them succeeded, the Jaguar Cup could disappear forever this time. It's too great a risk."

José's mom nudged him forward, toward two men in tuxedos and a woman in a long, sleek black dress waiting at the other end of the velvet ropes. "Come on. It's a terrific show, even without the cup. Don't forget Alejandro's masks are here. And Sofia's drawings from the rain forest. And —"

"Welcome, my friends!" The woman in the black dress swooped in and ushered them through the museum's main lobby and into a waiting elevator.

"Sixth floor," the woman told Henry, who was standing by the buttons. She turned to Anna's mom. "You've gotten the news today, I trust?"

"About the Red Sox? Hmph," Henry's dad grunted.

The grown-ups started chatting in the back of the elevator while Henry pushed the button for the sixth floor. José felt the elevator give a jolt as it started to rise. He tugged at his collar.

"You nervous?" Anna asked him.

"Kind of." José didn't like talking to big groups of grown-ups, but after everything he'd faced in Costa Rica, he figured he could survive this.

The elevator dinged, and the black-dress lady stepped forward so her shiny black high heels were right next to José's too-tight brown dress shoes. Something jingled at her feet, and José's attention immediately landed on the ankle bracelet she wore. It had only one charm — a delicate silver jaguar.

José jerked his head up and slid over toward his mom as they all filed out of the elevator into a room full of more fancy-dress ladies and old men in suits, milling around with wine glasses.

"That lady's in the society?" José whispered.

His mom nodded and gestured toward the podium set up in the center of the atrium. They walked over to it, away from the crowd, while the black-dress lady introduced the others to some museum employees. "She's a descendant of Isabella Stewart Gardner."

"What was she talking about in the elevator?" Suddenly, her "news" seemed a lot more interesting.

"Goosen," his mom whispered. "There was news out of Amsterdam this morning. Police raided Goosen's mansion there last night, recovered millions — probably billions of dollars' worth of art — and arrested Goosen and his son."

"He has a *kid*?" José asked. It was impossible to imagine the steel-faced man from the zip line teaching somebody to ride a bike or pouring sippy-cups of juice.

"He actually has two sons who are all grown up. Henrick was arrested with him and the other one, Vincent Junior, hasn't been seen in years, ever since — Hello, Donald!" José's mom called over the top of his head, and he turned to see a gangly Asian man with a thin cap of wispy black hair rushing toward them.

"Maria!" he held out his skinny arms to hug her, then stood back and looked at José. "And this must be our young hero."

"Uh . . ."

"One of them," his mom said, smiling, and she waved over Henry and Anna. "Kids, this is Donald Zeng."

"A pleasure to meet you kids." The man reached out to shake Anna's hand, then Henry's and José's. A fat silver jaguar looked as if it were about to leap from the ring on his finger. He turned back to talk quietly with José's mom.

"This place is crawling with you-know-whats," Anna leaned over and whispered to José. "Is everybody in Boston a Silver Jaguar Society member?"

"Boston's full of rabble-rousers and scofflaws who won't keep the king's peace," Henry said.

José looked at him.

Henry shrugged. "It's from my game, Rogue Assassins for Liberty. Aunt Lucinda got it for me when she found out we were moving here."

"Are the kids ready?" The black-dress lady was back, pointing to the podium. Most everyone else was already seated.

"The kids are totally ready," Henry said, shoving José forward. Easy for him to say; they'd decided that Anna would welcome everyone and then José would explain . . . well . . . why the gold exhibit was missing its most famous piece.

Anna stepped up to the podium and unfolded the paper with her notes. "Good afternoon. We'd like to thank you for coming today, to see this exhibit that showcases the culture of Latin America hundreds of years ago. It's taken some interesting twists since its first installation in Washington, DC, this summer. You'll notice there are new pieces on display. They include handcrafted ceremonial masks." She gestured toward the case that held Alejandro's little devil masks. José was surprised Alejandro had agreed to let them go. Maybe he was trying to make up for losing the cup the last time it was supposed to be on display.

"You'll find a detailed interpretive panel with photographs and information on the great green macaw — a true treasure of Latin America that has survived the test of time. These birds were here when Columbus landed, and they remain today, though in dwindling numbers. We hope you'll read — and act — to protect these beautiful birds."

Anna cleared her throat. "You'll also find a replica of the historical golden cup that was scheduled to be on display. My friend José is here to explain why you won't see the real thing today."

She gestured toward him enthusiastically as if she expected everyone to clap about the fake cup. No one did.

José's mouth felt as dry as if he'd been licking the hot pavement outside. "Thanks." His voice cracked.

"As Anna mentioned, the cup you see in the exhibit today is not the one that archaeologists discovered in a seaside Costa Rican cave earlier this year. That cup . . ." He paused and looked at his mom for moral support. But she was looking down at her phone. During his speech? She was always reminding his dad how rude it was to check the weather radar on his phone in restaurants.

A man in the front row cleared his throat, and José continued. "That cup is now part of a special permanent display at the Gold Museum in San José. After the recent attempt to steal it, authorities decided that it should stay in Latin America, where the people who created it intended it to remain."

He looked down at his notes. Then looked back up. His mom was still staring down at her phone.

In fact, all over the room, people seemed to be pulling out their cell phones. There had to be nearly a dozen now, all frowning down at their screens. What were they doing? Texting their friends? *Don't bother with MFA exhibit. Skinny kid says real cup not here.*

"Like the great green macaw and the tradition of the Dance of the Little Devils, represented by the handcrafted masks you see here," José continued, "the cup is a symbol that represents the rich history and culture of Latin America. So we hope you'll enjoy the pieces that have joined this exhibit and understand why one is missing. Thanks."

They clapped. At least the ones who weren't on their phones did.

"You did a great job," José's mom told him when he found her at the hors d'oeuvres table. She had a stuffed mushroom in one hand and her phone in the other. She smiled, but her eyes were worried.

"What's going on?" José asked. "You were on your phone during my talk."

She sighed. "It's Goosen."

Henry sidled up to them. "Dude, Goosen *texted* you during the talk? That's wicked."

José's mom shook her head and smiled a little. "No, it wasn't him. It was a society member in Amsterdam. Goosen escaped out the window of a moving police van on the way to court a few minutes ago."

"Whoa!" Henry's mouth fell open.

"Seriously?" Anna whipped out her notebook.

"He got *away*?" José must have looked terrified because his mother reached out and squeezed his shoulder.

"This happened on the other side of an ocean, far away. We're all safe. And they'll find him." But she didn't look convinced of that.

"You know," his dad said. "I could go for an ice-cream cone at Quincy Market. Sound like a plan?"

"Are ties required at Quincy Market?" Henry asked, already loosening his collar.

"I don't believe they are," his aunt said, smiling.

"Then I'm in."

"Me, too!" Anna said, following Henry toward the elevator.

"Me three." José walked alongside his mom, who kept looking down at him, worried.

"It'll be okay," she whispered. "You're safe."

For right now, José thought. But he didn't say that out loud. Today was their day, a celebration of ice cream and great green macaws, of Alejandro's masks and Sofia's drawings, and even though it was far away, a celebration of the Jaguar Cup.

José remembered the feeling of holding it in his hands. Its smooth warmth. Its heaviness. He remembered the promise he'd whispered at his reflection in the gold. He felt the cup's presence, even though it was half a continent away, and in his heart he knew two things were true.

He would meet Vincent Goosen again someday.

And when that day came, José would keep his promise.

AUTHOR'S NOTE

One of my favorite things about writing books for kids is doing research. Usually, my research begins in the library, with stacks and stacks of books and folders full of websites that I've bookmarked. But when I'm working on a story like *Hide and Seek*, where the setting is so fascinating and so important to the plot, research also involves getting on an airplane and spending time in the place that my characters explore.

I still remember reading about the rain forest when I studied ecosystems with my third-grade teacher, Mrs. Fox. We decorated construction-paper folders for all the places we'd study in that unit, from the desert to the tundra. But the rain forest was my favorite. How could one place on Earth be so full of so many plants and animals, so supercharged with life? And I remember telling my parents that I wanted to visit a rain forest and see it all for myself. "Maybe someday," they'd say.

"Someday" arrived in the summer of 2010. As part of my research for *Hide and Seek*, my family and I spent four days at Selva Verde Lodge in the rain forest of Costa Rica. Our room was deep in the forest, up on stilts so that it didn't flood in the rains that came every afternoon.

Almost all of the animals that José, Anna, and Henry encounter in their adventure were part of our adventure, too. We awoke at five o'clock in the morning to howler monkeys roaring to claim their territory and toucans squabbling over breakfast, high in the trees.

We saw leaf cutter ants and stingless bees and blue morpho butterflies, golden orb spiders, fruit bats, and a male glass frog, camouflaged perfectly to blend in with the eggs he was guarding.

Fortunately, there was no fer-de-lance lurking outside our room, but we did come upon one of the deadly snakes in the middle of the trail during one of our afternoon hikes.

Our local guide, Alex, had advised us to "just walk around" the less aggressive venomous snakes we saw, much as Sofia tells her new friends when they come across a hog-nosed viper. But when we met up with the fer-de-lance, Alex had us all step back until he was able to coax the snake off the trail with a very long stick. We waited and watched as it slithered up over a branch and deeper into the forest.

Like José, Anna, Henry, and Sofia, we also crossed a swinging, swaying bridge over the river.

The bridge led from our lodge to the primary forest, where our guide, Alex, took us on a long hike to a giant old almendro tree.

We marveled at the size of the tree and all the different animals that relied on it for food and shelter. I couldn't resist; I climbed right inside to listen to the quiet dark and bat squeaks.

The one creature we never saw, though we longed to spot one, was the great green macaw.

I was sad about that until I realized that it gives me a perfect reason to return to this amazing place. It is everything that third-grade me dreamed it would be.

To read more about our time in Costa Rica and to see my wildlife photos, visit my Pinterest board, *Hide and Seek Resources*: http://pinterest.com/katemessner/ hide-and-seek-resources/

IN MANHUNT, the Serpentine Princes pull off their biggest crime yet, an international museum heist that spans the globe. Check out this special sneak peek!

When the Louvre finally reopened after the heist, Anna, Henry, and José wandered through the European art halls with their Paris guide, Hem. He seemed relieved to find two Vermeer paintings on the walls. "Thank God," he said. "*The Astronomer* and *The Lacemaker* are safe."

But not far away, one of Hem's other favorites had been sliced out of its frame. "It was one of Corot's sailboats," Hem said. "A really spectacular one, too. The sky behind it was all moody." He paused and lowered his voice. "I have this weird feeling that Vincent Goosen and I have the same taste in art."

José nodded slowly. "Like Harry Potter and Voldemort. They're on opposite sides, but there's this weird connection, and in some ways they have a lot in common."

"So wait," Henry said. "You think Goosen is stealing his favorite stuff?"

"I do." Hem took a deep breath. "And I have an even worse feeling that he's not quite finished."

"Why do you say that?" José asked.

Before Hem could answer, an alarm sounded, whooping through the gallery so loud Henry thought it might shatter the glass cases. "Attention, please, visitors. Due to a security breach, we must evacuate the museum immediately."

ABOUT THE AUTHOR

KATE MESSNER is the author of *The Brilliant Fall of Gianna Z.*, winner of the E. B. White Read Aloud Award for Older Readers; *Sugar and Ice*; *Eye of the Storm*; *Capture the Flag*; *Sea Monster's First Day*; *Over and Under the Snow*; and the Marty McGuire chapter book series. A former middle-school English teacher, Kate lives on Lake Champlain with her family and loves reading, walking in the woods, and traveling. Visit her online at www.katemessner.com.